GOOD FENCES

GOOD FENCES

A NOVEL

ERIKA ELLIS

RANDOM HOUSE
NEW YORK

Library of Congress Cataloging-in-Publication Data
Ellis, Erika.
Good fences / Erika Ellis.—1st ed.
p. cm.
ISBN 0-679-44876-4
I. Title.
PS3555.L59494G66   1997
813'.54—dc21   96-46328

Good Fences is a work of fiction. Names, characters, places, and in-
cidents are the product of the author's imagination or are used ficti-
tiously. Any resemblance to actual events, locales, or persons,
living or dead, is entirely coincidental

Random House Website address: www.randomhouse.com

Manufactured in the United States of America
2   4   6   8   9   7   5   3
First Edition

To Mom, Granny, Muriel M.,
and my darling Trey
for knowing I was a writer before I did

GOOD FENCES

1972

GOOD FENCES

"Stormy, set the table! And Hilary, come stir some butter into these beans like I told you fifteen minutes ago. I'm not running my mouth for my health." Mabel mashed a fork against the side of her pan of gravy. Flour lumps popped up like life preservers, she'd have to run it through the strainer. Tom would be home from work any minute now, and looking for his supper.

"Girls! What did I say! And Tommytwo—Tommytwo?—lotion those ashy legs. Your daddy will have a fit." She scowled from one end of the kitchen to the other, searching for the Accent salt. She'd swear she'd seen that shaker yesterday when she was doctoring the leftover kielbasa. Might have even shook a bit in along with the rest of that bag of peas. Mabel closed her eyes and tried to whiff it out somehow. Mabel was famous around here for her sniffing power.

There was Luisa-next-door's perfume still hanging in the

air from early this morning. No such thing as a closed gate, as far as Luisa was concerned. Today the woman had practically tripped over the children trying to get inside Mabel's kitchen to take up where she'd left off yesterday bragging about her new carpet, her new wall-to-wall. "And zee baby's room!" Baby pee on the carpet—no matter, they'd paid the forty dollars extra for a special protective coating. Mabel would be getting her own wall-to-wall carpet as soon as she could tease it out of the monthly budget, protective coating and all.

"Mommy, can we—may we—wait until *Felix the Cat* is over?" Stormy hopped side to side in the kitchen archway on her matchstick legs, eyes batting, dimple flashing. More charm than Rodney Allen Rippy. Mabel had this twin's number.

"Yes you may, but—" Before she could tack on conditions, the child was gone. Best always to tack on conditions. Stay up an extra half an hour playing Mr. Potatohead on a Friday night, be prepared to mop the bathroom floor Saturday morning, no lip. Leeway spoiled children, Mabel was a firm believer. If it weren't for Tom and his new 1970s child-raising philosophies brought home from the white folks at work, all three of these kids would have their own special patch on their behind where they best preferred to get swatted. Now Tina-two-doors-down, on the other hand, she had those boys of hers spoiled to the point where they expected a bedtime snack brought to them every night on a certain tray. Butter cookies, too, as chunky as those boys already were at ten years old.

Mabel patted her hands down her apron pockets, stuck her fingers inside and wiggled them, just on the long shot. A quarter container of Accent salt couldn't have simply disappeared, not unless Mabel was losing her mind. She patted around for it inside the coupon drawer. Yes, Tom and his philosophies. What was that nonsense he used to pretend to read out of the Dr. Spock book, with his droll sense of humor. Only the extremely niggerish beat their kids, he said, some silliness like that. Some of the mess Tom said plus a quarter would buy half a cup of coffee.

She could easily have found herself married to a man with a lot more bad habits than a strange sense of humor. Mabel could have found herself married to another Charlie Johnson. Detours to the racetrack each and every payday, and poor Tina's impacted wisdom tooth digging itself deeper down into her jawbone every day the Lord sent. Mabel reminded herself to phone that girl later on this afternoon. Charlie had some new job he was up for with better insurance. Which he'd need if Tina kept feeding those boys all that sugar.

Mabel stirred her gravy, mashed the lumps. She'd married a good man, all right, a man with his priorities in order, a man with drive. Still the only negro ever hired in his firm, but after ten years his good word was starting to hold some weight among those bigots when other negro applicants came along. And Tom was a fine father to his children. Monopoly! Battleship! I ought to buy stock in Toys "R" Us, Tom had joked last Christmas, pride ringing out above the babies' wheezes from their new plastic clarinets.

"Butter in the beans, Mommy?" Stormy twirled back into the kitchen. Mabel was going to do even better by these children, just as soon as she figured out how to juggle a little extra out of her weekly money. Dance lessons for the girls, and Tom thought karate lessons might toughen up Tommy-two. Mabel was still keeping an eye on that aluminum siding, even though they'd had to miss the special sale. One little boost from monthly savings on the heat bill would give them the safety ledge they needed. Where was that pamphlet from Sears, she'd meant to stick it on the refrigerator under the Rainbows and Dreams magnet.

"Daddy's home!" The Lord got his money's worth out of these children's ears all right. She heard the station wagon putter into the carport, rasping and hissing like a fussy old woman. Mabel wiped her hands on a dishcloth, satisfied she'd done her job. Kids were clean, table was set, dinner was just about ready to go right on the table.

The screen door flew open and in came Tom, footsteps quicker than usual after a long day's work. Not that Tom Spader was known for taking his sweet time. Man could walk a mile through drizzle and not get wet. But tonight, something was not quite right about the way he stood there with chest pumping in the kitchen archway, hands swatting at his knotted tie.

He dropped his briefcase and stood there, tongue lolling in his mouth like limp fingers as he tried to speak. "Those S.O.B.s finally gave him a heart attack" whipped back and forth through Mabel's brain on its own as Tom stood there huffing like a man on the run. Tommytwo's little skinny arms wound around her legs.

"Television," Tom finally managed to sputter, and a smile lit his face like summer sunshine. "I'm on *television!*" He skidded through the kitchen, slapping countertops on his way.

"Daddy's on television!" screeched the children, dancing after him into the den.

"Thank you, Jesus." Mabel stumbled after her family. "Thank you, Joseph, thank you, Mary." It was just like Tom Spader to terrify somebody half to death spreading good news.

The children snaked on the den rug and Mabel knelt, flipping channels. Tom hunched forward on the brown couch, stabbing his finger toward each image. Good-looking as he was, it was natural he'd wind up on television. Except she wasn't finding him on either Two, Five, or Seven. She checked Channel Thirteen, then started back at Two.

"It'll be at the Federal Building. Me, Joe, a couple other associates." Tom yanked at his tie, legs hopping like rabbits even as he sat. Trouble? mouthed Mabel over the kids' heads. It couldn't be trouble, not with him running through the house that way. Surely not trouble, not the way he'd lit up so bright. Trouble? she mouthed again, a little more anxious. Tom said Shhh, testier than need be. He waved her silent, his green eyes steady, glaring at the set.

Mabel wondered who told Tom that lie about being on television. Probably one of his so-called buddies upstairs in

Legal. Set the table, she whispered to the girls, flipping the channel once more for good measure. Just as Mabel started through the channels one last time, Tom clapped a palm against his thigh. "That's it! The Federal Building!"

The children stared transfixed at their daddy on the local news like a movie star, and Mabel couldn't help but hug her knees and grin. Those were her Tom's shoulders—and sometimes she forgot what a big man he was—wide as they pleased, wider than any of the other men, all the rest white men, glowing out of the television set. The reporter pointed the microphone at Tom's chin and asked some mumbo jumbo about defense strategy.

"Show Daddy some more!" yelled Hilary.

"Hush!" cried Tom, halfway hopped off the couch, stabbing a finger toward one edge of the screen. "Now here, watch. Take a look at Joe Klein's face when he gets it! Watch it, watch how he freezes up when he realizes the sonofabitch wants to hear what a black man has to say! Son of a bitch!"

"Son of a bitch," giggled the children. Mabel lifted one eyebrow at them and scrubbed her tongue with play soap. She didn't care if their daddy was on TV, no child of hers had any business cussing, they knew better than that.

"Sources say your client will submit a plea of not guilty to the arson charge although there were witnesses." Mabel could barely hear the reporter's next question for Tom's stamping his feet and his howls of laughter mixing with the children's whoops. The nerve of that Joe Klein. Two years now since he took over the other desk down in Legal Research. His specialty was doing the complaining while Tom did the work, even though Joe had some high-up uncle on the company letterhead poised to pull strings if he ever decided to give up drinking. It'd been two years since the first time Joe'd rattled on to Mabel about his Meg's Swedish meatballs, which he seemed to feel obliged to do each and every time Mabel phoned. From the first, she'd realized all that useless chatter served to smooth his own ruffled chest hairs over having to answer his own phone down there. She'd always felt sorry for him herself, until now. Joe had the nerve to grit his teeth when he saw the microphone was angled at Tom, not him. Next time Mabel saw that wife of his, she was going to give her a good piece of mind about those nasty brown curtains she'd hung in the fellows' office. If anybody had the seniority to hang curtains after ten long years, it was Mabel.

"My client acted in self-defense," Tom told the reporter. A snapshot filled the screen of Tom's client in his dental office, looking more like the local hero than an arsonist, with a silver pin in his tie and sporting three white hairs combed sideways over his pink egghead. Looked almost pleased with himself. The next picture was of the boys who'd been burned, two raggedy, nappy-headed boys who looked like they didn't know what had hit them.

"Is Dr. Silver aware that there were eyewitnesses, including the two currently hospitalized teens and other residents present when the doctor set the apartment building on fire, whose sworn statements strongly contradict—"

"Those young men were eighteen years old, Bob, hardly 'teens.' And neither can we call a slew of illegal squatters 'residents,' can we?" Tom spoke directly into the camera. "A gang of unemployed vagrants took up residence in the doctor's property and refused to evacuate despite three court orders. This well-respected doctor is being victimized, held without bail . . ." Tom seemed born for television, handsome as he was. He stood ahead of the pack, his colleagues stuck behind for once like backup singers, craning their necks to get into the picture. The children shrieked and punched each other in the bellies until Mabel said Hush.

"One last thing, Attorney Spader. Would you give us a comment about the swelling dismay within the black community, epitomized by yesterday's firebombing of a local drugstore?" Scaredycat, thought Mabel, still pissing their pants about the riots. The reporter pointed his microphone back at Tom, who was grinning now, although Mabel couldn't exactly figure out what was so funny. And while Mabel didn't know much about the legal world and defense strategies, something about that grin didn't seem right, not with two boys hovering near death, even two boys on the wrong side of the law. She shut her eyes for a moment, let it pass.

"My children also get a bit dismayed when I punish one of them for breaking our house rules," Tom said. "So I punish them a bit more severely the next time."

Tom's shoulders squared inside his suit jacket, nearly filling the screen. What we need is a bigger TV set, Mabel told herself, a twenty-four-inch like the Rodriguezes' next door. Truth be told, she wasn't sure she liked the idea of Tom becoming television spokesman for this particular case. They ought to ask him about the corporate mergers he normally did all the research for, not just about this fluke cops-and-robbers case for some big client's dentist son-in-law. A smile was dancing around the reporter's mouth now too, eyes twinkling above his Back to you, Hank.

The children gave their daddy a standing ovation and Mabel clapped too, as relieved that it was over as she was proud. She hadn't thought it right at first, Tom defending an admitted arsonist who'd nearly killed two sleeping boys, no matter what crime they'd committed. Two negro boys, at that.

Is it right, she'd been fool enough to wonder aloud the day the firm offered Tom the case. Of course it's right, Tom had snapped back, and who could blame him. Joe Klein wasn't the only one itching to leave that basement office. All these years, watching a half dozen Joe Schmoes packing their desk blotters and promising to pull strings soon as they got settled in upstairs, of course that would weigh heavy on a man as ambitious as Tom. Swearing they'd spread the word about the good work Tom Spader was doing down in the basement, then treating Tom like the shoeshine man when they passed him in the lobby. If she had any sense at all, she'd be thanking Jesus for sending them this arsonist. She forced herself to feel grateful as she watched Tom pack Stormy's and Tommy-two's little skinny legs around his waist and heft them, neighing and galloping into the kitchen.

Half hour later, Hilary was the last child at the table, lips poked out so far over her cold beans that Mabel had to clamp her teeth together to keep from busting out laughing. Of all her children, Mabel got the biggest kick out of little Miss Hardhead. Child was stubborn as a mule, as Mabel's ma would say, and as bad as any boy. The little pile of lima beans was already congealed.

"You'd better eat those beans," threatened Mabel, wiping off placemats.

Her daddy'd see to her in a minute, no doubt about that. Nobody wasted food in the Spader household. There were hungry children right here in Hamden, Connecticut, who would have loved some good beans. For the moment, Tom was still absorbed in his cigarette. It never failed to startle people to see a man that energetic sitting stock-still, caught in his trances. Folks who knew Tom Spader knew a man on the run, always moving, arranging. He was different from other husbands, a breed apart from her daddy, rocking in his porch chair, yelling Who That! if a truck drove by. Get her daddy his playing cards and his bottle of cough syrup set down on the plank by his leg. It didn't take much more than that to keep most men Mabel grew up around satisfied, especially on their time off. But not Tom Spader, no ma'am. He was a man on the move. Even moments like this when he sat stock-still, his temples throbbed same as if a bomb was ticking inside his skull.

"Your brother and sister get to play Mr. Potatohead until bedtime," Mabel told Hilary, straightening three empty chairs. "You don't."

"The fellow knew my name," said Tom, so quietly Mabel barely caught it. His plate was empty except for tissuey squares of torn-up napkin, which Mabel would have to scrape now, instead of rinse. He set a bad example sometimes, especially for someone as hardheaded as little Miss Smartypants over there.

"Ain't going to eat the yucky beans," sniffed Hilary. "Hate beans."

"I know I didn't hear you say 'ain't.' " Mabel swabbed at Tom's placemat with the dishrag as he sat there still as a statue, intent on the smoke disappearing into the light fixture. The crease in his shirt was blade sharp, even this time of night.

"He called me Attorney Spader. How about that." Tom caught Mabel's hand, tossed her dishcloth aside. One glance at Hilary and the beans were gone and so was she.

"Attorney Spader, did you hear him?"

"I heard him," said Mabel. "Attorney Spader, just like that."

"How about that?" said Tom. He snatched Mabel down right across his lap, caught her cheeks in his palms and kissed her like a newlywed. She giggled, cussing the thighs God gave her for plumping out like Christmas hams against his slacks at a time like this.

"Attorney Spader! On television!"

"Shoot, that's no surprise . . . a man like you," Mabel whispered into his freshly cut curls, glad to see him so tickled. The barber had cut his hair so low this week his head felt like the bristles on her good brush.

"Things are finally starting to pull together. This case

could be the one to start the ball rolling . . ." His eyes gleamed toward the ceiling. She shifted her weight to be less of a burden on his legs.

"And make the walls come tumbling down!" Couples always had their private jokes, the way Tina and Charlie up the block always did that routine about why waste the olive on the martini. Tom and Mabel only cracked their old joke about knocking down walls in private, since it wasn't the sort of joke meant for a belly laugh. It was more pathetic than funny: two Lovejoy kids, green as blades of grass, living in a cold-water flat in Brooklyn, wondering what in the world they'd gotten themselves into. Twin baby girls sharing not just a crib but a blanket, Tom and Mabel, with a bottomless Spam casserole, watching the cars out the window and pretending the whole world would someday be their oyster, as if this world could ever be some negro's oyster. This time, though, something about the line was pinching Tom's funny bone. He laughed himself hoarse, tears squeezing past those silk eyelashes, the knee she was perched on wobbling. She shifted her entire weight onto one ankle to make herself light as a feather, and stayed that way long after her behind began to cramp up.

———

The very first day Mabel saw Tom Spader was that same day all those fresh strawberries ended up in Ma's kitchen. Sweetened every drop of air in the house. First time Mabel'd ever seen strawberries. Bright red fruit, pulpy as cut tomato, wiped out all traces of Daddy's foot ointment. Mabel drank the sweet smell in.

Mabel was sweet sixteen, but a young sixteen. Still playing with dolls, still barely dared thought about kissing anybody. So young and silly she genuinely believed there must be something magical about a bowl of fruit that could cover up the smell of Daddy's feet. All those strawberries, so fragrant and plump, squishing in their own juice, good Lord in heaven. A potato bug had ten times the common sense of Mabel Agnes Turner, Aunt Hattie used to say. Too dumb to see those strawberries were a week past ripe.

"Mabel Agnes," Ma had called from the sink that morning, back arched as high as a wet cat's. "Mabel Agnes!" she'd screeched, though Mabel was standing not two feet away. That white woman Ma hated so bad, Mrs. Whoosit with all that curly brown hair, owed Ma four dollars. Been owed it. Then had the nerve to send somebody's child around to Ma's house with that bucket of strawberries. Ma was in a rage that day, elbows whisking through the air like blades as she soaped her pots.

"Mabel Agnes Turner," Ma hissed, and Mabel's whole body shot through with terror. Lovejoy, Illinois, was a colored town, and folk whipped youngsters just because back in those days, circling the switch above their heads like a lasso. At home, in the street, didn't matter. Boy'd be big as town hall, trudging out to the stink tree to slice off the very switch his mama'd use to whup his own behind. The back door stood open for breeze that hot July day and if Mabel'd been another type of girl, she'd have tried to run to China. It was those fat, pretty berries even more than the angry brown grooves dug across Ma's forehead that kept her glued in her place.

"Mabel Agnes."

"Yes, Ma?" The smell of strawberries wrapped around Mabel's neck like a fox-fur throw.

"Stir me up my starch!"

Mabel held tight to the fork and whisked that starch fast as the devil, practically whipped up meringue. And the whole while she fought not to swoon as she stood there drowning in sweet perfume. White folk sure knew how to live.

"I advanced that white woman four dollars," Ma muttered into the silver soap bubbles.

"Yes, Ma," Mabel said back quick. Everybody knew colored folk didn't do any such thing as advance money to white folk. White woman owed her, that was all. Most likely would never pay her, either, not after sending over that big bucket of strawberries.

" 'Member of her family' my foot," sneered Ma. "Should of said my Good Mornings and left it at that, no matter how much conversation that woman wanted out of me."

"Yes, ma'am," said Mabel, although any fool knew better than to rile white folk on purpose, for four dollars or four hundred. At sixteen years old, Mabel Agnes had never traveled more than a nickel bus ride out of Lovejoy, but she knew white folk same as if the Turners kept one living in the front room. She'd seen the whip marks snaking down Old Man Apron Wilson's back. And teachers would tell you straight out, the only white man you don't have to call Mister is Jesus. But honey, they'd all tell you in that very next breath, don't you nevvver, never trust them.

"Strawberries! Nerve of that white woman. A bucketful of strawberries, half of 'em mush. Good fences make mighty good neighbors when it comes to these low-down crackers, you hear me, child?" But it was Ma herself who'd set a bowl of the strawberries on the table, the slightest bit off center.

"Best eat 'em before they rot." Ma cut her eyes at the bowl then turned back to her pots. Ma was famous for her moods. "But don't get used to it," she spat over her shoulder as Mabel crammed the fruit into her mouth.

Mabel Agnes Turner was more dog biscuit than sugar cookie, she knew that for a fact. Boys gathered around the barbershop didn't call out to her rump and legs, they pointed out that her arms were as thick and black as blood sausage, and that her elbows stayed silver despite the grease she slathered onto them. Play deaf, she and Shirley Hilliard hissed at each other as they passed those boys by, staring straight ahead into outer space. But not a soul on earth could have told Mabel Agnes she wasn't the best-looking thing ever to grace the streets of Lovejoy that Saturday afternoon on her way to the show, despite the fact that she was still tracing strawberry pulp out from between her teeth with a fingernail. Had a quarter in her pocket, too. Yes, Mabel was ravishing the Saturday afternoon she first saw Tom Spader.

There was a Tyrone Power picture showing at the Harlem

that day, and Tyrone Power was Mabel's idea of suave. Shirley—crazy Shirley Hilliard—was late meeting up. The line of folks snaked down the length of Madison Avenue, and everybody in it seemed to be talking loud about nothing. Fast Renetta Blount was telling somebody that she'd heard somebody tell somebody that somebody else's nephew was coming for a stay, and how she sure hoped he was good-looking. The barber had pulled his chair out in the middle of the road to mind folks' business better. His customer was wiggling about, getting his scalp nicked.

Big and John both worked full-time jobs at the stockyard with Daddy now, so Mabel's family was as good as rich, and there was always change in the jar for Mabel to see a matinee. She might have even been jingling an extra nickel in her pocket that day, for Cracker Jack. For whatever reason, Mabel was in seventh heaven that afternoon, from early on.

But then she spotted Pea Pie Persons, this side of the barber, cutting up with the other boys like the royal fool that he was. Pea Pie was the ugliest, blackest thing in town, with enough peasy hairballs on his neck to break a comb, thicker than a swarm of honeybees. Might have even had a rag full of potatoe slices tied around his throat that day, curing his cold. His folks were fresh from Alabama and boy did it ever show. Worst part about Pea Pie Persons was that he had a crush on Mabel, and the whole town knew it. She whipped back around quick before he caught her with his dull, flat eyes.

Her dilemma was, she had to find Shirley Hilliard before Boscoe Brown, whose job it was to take tickets at the matinee, then smooth them out for the evening show, unhooked the red rope and let the line start moving. Pea Pie spotting her would have ruined her whole Saturday. It was Big and John's fault she had developed her secret talent.

Most folks who knew about Mabel Agnes just said God got his money's worth out of her nose, and left it at that. But her brothers used to razz her about her sniffing powers. They'd call her Fido and have her sniff things out around the house. By sixteen, she'd taught herself to suck in a whole headful of smells without even twitching. She'd roll the odors around in her mouth the way a fisherman sorted through his nets, keep some, discard most. All her life, Mabel had never told a soul she smelled Tom Spader before she ever saw him.

Yes, she went sniffing for the scent of Shirley Hilliard's mama's tea-rose oil, which Shirley always snuck a little bit of behind her ears for the Saturday matinee, and instead she found Tom Spader. His unfamiliar scent stuck out from among the kids in line's hot handfuls of coins and dirty paper money like a sunflower out of snow. She trembled when she found him, she couldn't help it. Hugged herself and just stood there in the street shaking like a bowl of rice pudding.

Who's boy is that, folks were whispering all around her. Don't look like nobody's boy I know. I got cousins that yella in Chicago, said Pea Pie in his high-pitched voice, but folks knew better than to pay him any mind. I got cousins every bit as yella as that boy and they ain't nothin'. As he got closer, she saw the boy could have been Billy Eckstine's younger brother, he was that good-looking. Fast Renetta

Blount was shoving folks aside, mouth dropped open wide enough to catch flies. Mabel stood perfectly still, convinced he was coming straight toward her, that in fact she was drawing him to her, breathing him in. It was a miracle her lungs didn't burst that day, so hard was she sucking in air.

He was the fastest-moving boy she'd ever seen, which could have been part of what folks were staring at. Folk didn't move that quick in Lovejoy. Walk that fast and you'd eventually end up having to sit and wait for your buddy. He was clearly dirt-poor, the kind of poor that folks bragged about having survived. His suitcase was more tape than cardboard and more string than tape. He held it like a weapon as he stopped to stare back at the onlookers.

"I got cousins yella as you in Chicago, and they ain't nothin'!" shouted Pea Pie when the boy was directly in front of him, thumping his chest so hard that potato slices rained down from the rag at his neck. But that new boy, shoot, he just stood there, spine tight as a pin, green eyes snapping. Then he curled his mouth into a sneer and thumbed the sweat off his forehead and flung it to the ground. Might as well have shot a wad of spit at the Harlem's marquee. "Is all the rest of you as dumb as that boy?" he cried out, chin jutted forward as if he expected a reply.

Pea Pie sprang toward the boy like a Joe Louis windup puppet gone haywire, and Tom Spader pounced. Mabel Agnes stared, bewitched, sure she was witnessing something connected to the call of the wild. It was no mere boys' fight, there was nothing anybody but Mother Nature could have done to stop it. The entire brawl couldn't have lasted more than a good two minutes from start to finish, but it left the whole crowd gasping for breath.

"Dumb monkey deserves what he got," she heard the boy mutter as he picked up his suitcase and dusted off his pants. Miraculously, she'd been thinking that exact same thing about Pea Pie in those exact same words. Mabel Agnes managed to smile broadly as the new boy passed her by, positive he'd never notice someone like her. She watched his tight, straight spine steer him up Monroe Street. Aretha could have sung it, about the fires burning deep down in a woman's soul.

Daddy said the only way that uppity Spader boy could court his baby girl was over his dead body. Boy had finagled himself the evening shift over at the slaughterhouse, which gave Daddy the opportunity to watch him close. Boy thought he was too smart for his own good. Never played the dozens with Daddy and Jimmy Newt and the rest of them at breaktime, kept his head stuck in schoolbooks. "Al-gebrey," Daddy sneered. Swept faster than a demon besides, messing up everyone's pace. Nothing uglier than a colored man flunking for crackers, trying to climb headfirst into the boss man's pocket, Daddy swore, jaw popping with fury.

Ma, who'd carried on conversations with herself as long as Mabel could remember, began keeping up a low mumble about Tom Spader. Folks were suspicious of that boy for no reason, she'd mumble beneath her breath as she helped Daddy rub on his foot ointment. Tom Spader was a fine boy, a straight-A student, a credit to the race, she'd tell herself as she handed Daddy and the boys their plates of spoonbread and greens. Boy got more on his mind than you bunch of small-time negroes, Ma'd fuss at the dog as she rocked in her porch chair. Daddy whistled loud beside her and dealt solitaire onto a tray. Mabel woke one night to the sound of a rag wiping a dish so loud it screeched through the thin bedroom wall.

"—a credit to the race!" Ma said, voice raised in the kitchen.

"That nappyheaded Pea Pie'll do her just fine," Daddy said. Through the wall, Mabel could hear him flipping through the feathery pages of Ma's *Jet* magazine, too fast to be actually reading it.

"No harm if he sees her home from church!"

"When I'm in my grave," said Daddy.

Ma slammed the wet dishrag down.

"Hear me good," Ma shouted, and a saucer smacked against her prized Formica. "We both know it's God's honest truth. She's as black as a skillet! And got a nose so flat it's a wonder she can even breathe! And she's got the common sense of a peach pit besides. There's no line of Prince Charmings knocking down these doors. And when the day comes that she's out there boiling more white folks' damn white sheets, what you gonna tell her? What?"

Daddy cleared his throat.

"What?"

Daddy scraped the chair across the kitchen floor and left Ma in there fussing to herself. Mabel had never hated her daddy before that moment, nor loved Ma so. Smelly clouds of hot foot ointment floated underneath Mabel's door as Daddy passed by on his way to the back room. Years later, in the sixties, when the police gassed those protestors down South, Mabel would stay glued to the set, remembering Daddy's stinking feet, and humming right along to their "We Shall Overcome."

Ma's front room stayed quiet that first Sunday Tom Spader came courting, as quiet as a wake. Aunt Hattie, who'd invited herself over, sat beside Ma, holding knitting in her lap to camouflage mannish hands, eyes trained on Tom. Daddy's shiny black shoes were stretched out to the center of the room like guard dogs. He popped his knuckles and his neck, each rude noise the same as a cuss. But Ma was the one Mabel couldn't quit staring at. She hadn't even known Ma owned earrings, let alone a pair with glass dripping off them supposed to look like rubies. The air was heavy with words only a fool would have had the nerve to speak.

"Who your mama?" Aunt Hattie finally said.

"She's dead," Tom Spader said, voice hard as rock salt.

"How?"

"Mabel Agnes, pour this boy some more ice tea, you weren't raised in a barn. And Hattie, why you always got to be so nosy?" Ma sat sewing a sleeve onto John's work shirt and humming church songs, looking as content as if she'd been shown a glimpse of heaven. Mabel'd kept pouring ice tea as if she were the same old obedient Mabel Agnes she'd always been. As if her babydoll's dress in the back bedroom didn't already have a gold engagement ring nestled inside the hem.

"Gittin' late," Daddy said when the clock struck three.

"I'll be leaving," Tom answered back, eyes level with Daddy's but shoes tripping on the rag rug as Daddy snatched the front door open.

"Be sure to stop back by and visit." A note of falsetto in Ma's voice made everyone jump, but Ma coughed it out.

Mabel Agnes slipped back to her bedroom and bit out the stitches of her doll's hem. Licked saliva into her big knuckle and forced the ring down, then back up, on, then off, mulling over her pending marriage.

The problem was never that she didn't love Tom Spader with all her heart. It was just that he made her a little nervous. Watching those green eyes of his focused dead across the Missouri River as he told her he was the man going to end colored folks' losing streak, she'd felt scared. Moonlight's dabbling the river, she'd said, hoping some poetry would shift the tension. Dappling, he'd corrected, clasping her hand with a tenderness that made her heart skip but never moving his eyes back from the distant bank. Then he'd taken the ring out of his pocket and told her she was the one, they were to be married. She knew she was the luckiest girl in the world, but somehow she still felt jumpy.

She used to sew the ring into her dollbaby dress in the mornings and pick it out at night to wear while she slept. Within two weeks she'd had the primary stages of gangrene, and one of the Bledsoe boys had to drive them over to the colored clinic in East St. Louis. Scared as Ma must have been to have a child with a hand swollen three times its normal size, she lit up like firecrackers the minute Mabel told her about the engagement ring. Ma's joy was so contagious that soon all three of them were bouncing in the cab of the Bledsoe truck, higher than driving over unpaved streets would have caused. Mabel still kept that ring, that piece of tin, upstairs in her jewelry drawer somewhere. She'd have to dig it out one of these days to show her girls.

————

Hair Day was always an ordeal, might as well get started. Mabel figured the good Lord must have been playing a practical joke when he sent her down twin girls so completely in her image she could have spit them right out of her mouth, hair like a barbed-wire cage from day one. Then, three years later, a boy with skin could have been a pound of God's sweet butter, prettier than the Michelangelo, head full of curls.

"Tommytwo, you can go play at Ball's house, but if Mrs. Odell asks you any more questions about your daddy's case you tell her you don't know. Woman ought to be ashamed of herself. You girls get your shirts off and take your hair out. Now."

"Aaaaaaawwwwwgggghh!"

Hilary sobbed like a motherless child, but Stormy wasn't doing a thing but putting on a show. If her mama didn't do her hair once a week she'd be fit to be tied.

"You first?" said Mabel. Stormy was already boosting herself up on the kitchen counter.

"Stick your head down. Neck feel all right?"

"Yes, Mommy." That hose attachment was the solitary special feature listed for the house back in '69. Talk about someone knowing how to make conversation, that real estate lady must have carried on for twenty-five minutes about the convenience of cleaning pots with that hose. And the whole while, Mabel wasn't thinking of a thing besides how easy that hose was going to make washing her baby girls' heads.

"Not getting a crook neck down there, are you?"

"No, Mommy."

Then, the moment they moved in, the darn thing broke. Hadn't been in the house more than a week. Typical of this house. Typical of Hamden. Lovejoy with a coat of wax and a few pale faces, that was all this city was.

Not that Mabel wasn't counting her blessings. Who would have ever expected it, Mabel Agnes Turner, whose mama used to wash white folks' sheets, a housewife. Little boy learning to play the violin in a mixed school. Husband a junior associate at a law firm, finally making a name for himself with his first big case. Still, she would have appreciated if that cheap hose attachment, this house's one frill, hadn't up and broken so easily.

"Mommy, what's a testicle?"

"Excuse me?"

"Why do the boys call Ball Odell a little black testicle head?"

"Girl, stick your head back under, there's some soap left in." The last thing Mabel felt like dealing with today was somebody's nosy little questions about sex. None of Stormy's business about that boy's nicknames. Nosy little twin, always poking that nose someplace it didn't belong. Mabel would crumble up and die if anything were to happen to any of her babies, crumble right up and die. She scooped water back behind Stormy's ears, aware that there was a tremble to her hands.

Three tiny babies, and Tom was getting threats from the so-called black community over that arson case. And she'd had to hear it on the news. Three tiny babies, and Mabel'd had to find out that people were plotting harm against her family over the local news. That man must have lost his mind. All he'd had to say when she'd called the office was that it was impotent threats from a bunch of crazy coons using those burned black boys finally passing away as an excuse to show their behinds. And to quit calling back because she was jamming up the line when there was a reporter trying to get through. It's good publicity for the case, he'd told her, and she could hear the grin in his voice as he said it. Any crazy coons try and mess with Tom Spader, cops had their number.

"Oh, Mommy, what's a testicle head, what's a testicle head," said Stormy, singing.

"I said stick under and stay that way. I ought to leave your hair and not straighten it this week." What infuriated Mabel the most was the way black folks made assumptions. All those negroes waving signs saying "Uncle Tom" Spader just because Tom was making the best of a bad situation ought to be thanking him instead. Any fool knew that a colored man with the word "Expert" floating beneath his chin on the nightly news was doing valuable race work, no matter what he was saying.

But these ignorant S.O.B.s wanted to crucify the man for having cut one corner. What was that fellow's name? That Stepin Fetchit. She'd bet black folk never called in death threats when it came time to make that Fetchit fellow the first negro in the Hall of Fame. Not that Mabel was comparing Tom . . . That wasn't what she'd meant one bit. Jesus up in heaven, it had been a long day already and it wasn't even noon yet.

"Mommy, can I have Shirley Temple curls today?"

"Don't even start."

"But you saiiiddd—"

"What makes you think you're getting curls? Who in the world said I have the time or the inclination to give you two curls today?"

"But you said I could have currrllls this week if I cleaned my side of the room and I cleeeeaned it!"

"I'll think about it."

"Mmmoom—"

"All right, that's it, no curls. Now go find your sister and tell her to get in here before I find my belt and give you both something to whine about. Run."

If Mabel was meant to get an ulcer, so be it. She was pushing the TV stand into the kitchen to turn on the news while she pressed Stormy's hair when the doorbell buzzed. Tina Johnson was a homing pigeon when she smelled burnt hair. And had the nerve to have on those new paisley hot pants she'd bought on sale at Howlands, freezing cold as it was outside. Mabel led her back to the kitchen, determined not to discuss what was on her mind.

Caroline Cartwright over on Temple had a mama-in-law who'd up and gifted them with a four-bedroom house—or was it five?—out in fancy Greenwich the day after Caroline turned up pregnant; that was big news, and she and Tina hadn't yet had their first conversation about it. Nice girl, that Caroline, although every salad she'd ever brought to a cookout had long blond hairs running through it, which Tina loved to mention. Yes, there was plenty to talk about without ever broaching the topic that was threatening to consume Mabel this awful day.

She put the teapot on and went ahead and told Tina the hot pants were a fine buy: lied, because it would take too much energy to start an argument over what grown women their age ought to be wearing. Her only desire was to finish ironing her girls' hair and to have this day come to a peaceful end. She settled Stormy's bony shoulders between her thighs and tried to concentrate on straightening out the child's wild bush of hair, but it was no use. A tear fell on a yank of freshly straightened hair. It was no use, none of it.

"Girl," said Mabel, unable to even get the word out. She put the comb down.

"I saw him. Just now on TV," said Tina, halfway talking and halfway whispering, and humming some of the words so the baby wouldn't understand.

"On the noon news?" Mabel stared back at Tina, eyes hot with tears. The soft tuft of straightened hair in her palm rolled back up like a potato bug as the tears soaked in. This little one's dream was to become a ballerina for her daddy. Loved her daddy so.

"They were announcing a panel discussion with him and some state legislature types," said Tina. She mouthed the rest: About preventing future riots.

"Oh Lord, no," said Mabel, putting the comb down, and Tina reached out and held her hand. They sat there in silence, tears streaming out of Mabel's eyes as she struggled to keep breathing steadily above the baby's resting head. Tina, sniffing companionably, stared her right in the eye. Tom Spader. On television. Cheeks bulging like a hyena's as he grinned back at some white politician trying to figure out how best to permanently hog-tie the black race. No doubt there'd be more death threats coming from these local negroes as the week wore on.

"Hey, Mommy?" Stormy's little voice piped up, somewhat muffled by Mabel's thigh. "Is the reason why Daddy is so popular because he smiles so much whenever he talks to white people on TV?"

Stormy had a talent for catching adults off guard. Just eight years old, but already knew exactly how this world worked and made no bones about it. Mabel put the comb on the table and peals of laughter shook her. Wheezing, contagious laughter. Tina howled and whipped off her wig and fanned herself with the bushy afro as long brown curls rolled down her back. Must have been ten good minutes before Mabel was able to pick the hot comb back up with a steady hand.

Stormy peeked at her Mickey Mouse watch. This was taking forever. She stared at the staticky hairs on Mrs. Johnson's neck as she rolled her head around laughing. She was beginning to get a funny feeling that not all girls had to get their hair straightened.

Her mother finally fingered the cool blue hair grease into Stormy's scalp. As a treat for having sat so still, Stormy was allowed to spend an hour with her hair loose, floating about her head like a fashion model's. She skipped down the hallway on tiptoes, the hair trailing behind her, floating through the air like strips of toilet paper. When she stopped short, it fell soft as feathers around her neck. She ran to the bathroom and posed in front of the mirror with her shirt pulled up. Mosquito-bite titties, she noted, as she did each day, the same as Tommytwo's.

Fly me, she said to the mirror, showing every single tooth like the lady in the commercial as she spoke. If the reason why Linda and Isabel and several others never ran inside very fast when it rained was that they didn't have to get their hair straightened, it just wasn't fair. They should have told her. Well, Stormy wasn't going to tell any of them her secret either. And her secret was better.

They're watching us every minute. She'd heard her daddy tell that to Tommytwo once, a long time ago. Nobody knew that she knew. She wasn't a hundred percent positive about who *they* was, but it might be the Martians. And if she was the only girl in her class that knew they were being watched, she would be the girl *they* would take on their spaceship. Stormy Spader: Spacegirl. Just like Judy Jetson.

"Baby, bring some fresh tea bags," Mabel's voice interrupted her thoughts from the kitchen.

"Yes, Mommy," Stormy called, flipping her hair so hard she fell over backwards.

———

Rainy springtime afternoons, listening to water crackling down the gutters, were Mabel's idea of paradise. And maybe when Tom got home they'd make their decision about that carpet they'd seen at Sears. She'd see how he was acting tonight. Because if he was acting anything like last night, there wouldn't be any problem at all with the Spaders using part of Tom's bonus to lay new carpet. Wall to wall to wall to wall.

She plumped up the cushion behind her, even considered unzipping the plastic covers and keeping them off permanently. The Spaders were coming into a whole new realm. Tom's big arson case was finally over and done with, thank goodness, and Mabel'd done the spring cleaning. Now they had summertime to look forward to, and spending that three thousand dollars. Millie Jackson cussed out a lover on the new turntable. Mabel did the Sweet Potato to the rhythm, right there on the couch.

The school bell rang out around the corner, always reminded Mabel of the Liberty Bell. Except three o'clock meant her liberty was coming to an end. Ball Odell was the first child to shoot down the sidewalk past Mabel's window—a showoff just like his mama, who couldn't get through a conversation without mentioning how small her feet were. Mabel didn't know why she even stayed friends with that woman. Patsy knew full well these kids nicknamed her boy Ball on account of his having been born with just the one testicle and didn't put a stop to it. And Patsy certainly was taking her sweet time stopping by to mention the Sears aluminum-siding truck that had been parked out front of Mabel's house all week. Bright orange truck, she couldn't have missed it.

You Patterson Avenue ladies are all something special, Mr. Meyer at the Stop & Shop always made a point of telling Mabel as he held her checks up to the light, his chubby little lips just a-licking. It would take a hard-boiled woman to not smile back. Patterson was a whole street of young mothers with hardworking husbands and good-looking babies, and now Luisa Rodriguez had her wall-to-wall carpet and Mabel finally had her aluminum siding, and even the Russian woman on the corner claimed to be making payments on a dining-room suite. They were all making progress, each at his own pace. So what if Mabel's husband had got a three-thousand-dollar bonus for winning a case. That didn't give anybody on this street a reason to start acting funny. Especially not some-one blessed with size-five feet like Patsy Odell.

The phone rang and caught Mabel off guard. She slid her

feet off the coffee table. "I was in Tom's litigation class at NYU Law," said a man talking fast. White man, nobody she knew. "Is he in? No? Just tell him I said he did an absolutely stunning job. Tell him Rudy says he's turned out to be one formidable litigator."

Rudy, Rudy, Rudy, repeated Mabel, scribbling the name at the bottom of the phone list. "Stunning," she wrote, "formidable." Folks in the law business certainly were impressed about Tom winning that arson case. Put some new glitch in the law books, according to Tom's new secretary. Kelly, Carrie, whatever that child's name was, she talked so much she'd let it slip about the rumor circulating the firm. Those people had surprised Mabel this time. A brand-new criminal division, and Tom to oversee it. Nowadays Tom ran right in and checked his phone messages each night. Mabel erased her messy writing and printed "formidable" just a little bit neater.

She propped a foot back up on the coffee table, gingerly. The firm had surprised her with their recent generosity, but they could just as easily snap their fingers and take it all away, so she'd best not scuff her furniture yet. Tom's colleagues and Patsy Odell. Mabel was getting quite a little list of people she'd better keep an eye on. Couldn't forget that Rodriguez grandmother who'd come storming over after they finally broadcast the jury's decision on the Spanish news two days late, handing back that cup of borrowed rice like it no longer had a place in her house. And not one word from Luisa since. One of these days Mabel would sit a few neighbors down about this arson case, and explain the subtleties. Although Lord knew some of these people were nobody's genius.

Truth was, Mabel hadn't discussed the court's decision with a soul, not even Ma. She'd call home and do some bragging when she figured out how to best explain it. And then there'd be Aunt Hattie and Big Sister Mercy in the yard behind the church, swearing they'd always predicted Tom Spader would do Lovejoy proud, lying through their teeth about the role they'd played in his upbringing. Maybe she'd use some of the bonus money to take the babies home for their first visit since back when Tommytwo was still a baby smelling up diapers. A root-beer bubble flew up Mabel's nose, made her smile.

"Blind man could see that boy was a credit to the race," she said aloud, talking cocky like Boscoe Brown. She could just see all the women standing around the schoolyard after the Easter pageant, bragging about having snatched their babies off their breast and sent them straight to school. Did you hear that boy of mine spell oxymoron? they'd say. Sure do know a whole lot more than how to fry bacon and roll logs, don't he? Even if it wasn't clear to the average individual at first glance, Tom Spader had done a whole town proud, a whole people.

Last night in bed, Tom had done some dreaming aloud in her ear. He'd talked so fast, his lip had snagged a roller sticking out from beneath Mabel's scarf. Where that man got his imagination was beyond Mabel. Fancy cars, Mercedeses and whatnot. Neighbors dressed in five-hundred-dollar tailored suits instead of Hardee's Hamburgers' manager uniforms like Rory Rodriguez's next door. He'd even teased her about hiring some help someday. She guessed he was teasing. Some help. What would Mabel need with some help. She sucked her triangular ice cube and beamed at the pictures that popped into her head: Mabel asking an English butler to please get the door, Mabel tasting gravy off a silver spoon while a French maid balanced the bowl. And a mansion in Greenwich, he'd said, which was when Mabel had begun to wonder how much gin was in his after-dinner drink. Tom had dropped off into one of his trances and Mabel had fallen into her own, weighing the pros and cons of buying a Crock-Pot.

They'd made love the way she liked it, lots of kissing and hugging, and it went on for quite a few minutes. Ninety-nine percent positive I'm going to head the division, Tom had whispered, his breath wetting her chin as his knees fought with the mattress. Go on, enroll the boy in karate class, go back to Bamberger's, buy yourself that leather purse. Walls go tumbling down! he'd cried out as he collapsed into his convulsions, and she'd worried that the children might wake up and come running in and catch her untwisting her nightgown. He'd drifted off to sleep right away without mentioning the shoes that matched the handbag, but she figured she'd pick them up too, as long as the sale was still on. Her Tom was an amazing man. She'd start spreading his good news come sundown, when long-distance rates were low. A credit to his race, she could hear Ma say.

"Hello?" she practically sang when the phone rang.

"Mrs. Spader?" A black man's voice grumbled like rolling thunder. Mabel's foot dropped off the coffee table.

"Mrs. Spader?" The man repeated, and Mabel could feel the blood coursing through the veins of her hand. Showing fear was the worst response, even if the man did know her name and number. Stay calm and explain, those boys' premature death was a god-awful tragedy, we must all learn and grow.

"Mrs. Spader?" Maybe it would never end, maybe these people would hold Tom winning that arson case against her family forever. And at the same time reap the benefits. White folks were hiring negroes all over town because of Tom Spader winning that case. Tom was right, these numbskulls wouldn't understand progress until it whacked them on their lazy behinds. Tom was just a cog in a wheel already rolling, that was what she wished she could scream back at them all. Tom was just a cog in a wheel, and the only negro cog, and they ought to be grateful! Tom was just a cog in a wheel!

"Tom is just a cog in a wheel!"

"Got the meat ready," said the man, and he had to repeat himself twice before Mabel remembered she had ordered a freezerful of beef cuts from the butcher. More sirloin than usual, and less hamburger. She pressed her cold glass to her forehead and told him to send the meat on over.

The deliveryman came right over and he packed the bundles into her freezer, and soon after, the children came hopscotching through puddles on the stoop. It turned out to be one of those quiet, real regular nights, although cool enough to turn the heat up. Tom came home with a nose all red and full of flu and said he'd had dinner, but wouldn't mind some pudding. Mabel never did find a free minute to call home.

————

"You're ADOPTED."

"Am not!" Tommytwo dodged spitballs.

"Mommy TOLD us you're adopted." Stormy bit off a fingernail and threw it at him. He dodged.

"Did not!"

His sisters were just mad that they had to play inside. Tommytwo told their mom he'd been having scary dreams again about monsters kidnapping his dad and then Mom started smoking Dad's pack of cigarettes and said she was sick and tired of small-minded Hamden people; then she got in the bathtub and told them to stay in the house all day or else she was going to whip them. The girls were just mad; he wasn't adopted. Duhhh.

"Are so. Mom told us last Saturday while we were getting our"—Hilary seized his arm and twisted it apart for a skin burn—"hair pressed." Tommytwo yelped, quietly so Mom wouldn't come.

"Stupid liars." His mom would have told him if he was adopted.

"Then you're calling our mom a liar." Stormy gave Hilary a nod and Hilary smacked him on the head. Mom had once forgotten to tell him about the puppy next door getting eaten by the German shepherd. Tears filled his eyes. Maybe he was adopted. The girls flicked him with their fingers and laughed at him trying not to cry.

"Let's put him in the refrigerator until he dies."

"Yeah!"

Both girls smothered him with kisses before opening the refrigerator and setting to work, moving milk and meatballs and a shelf rack and last night's macaroni casserole. Tommytwo stood there shrugging as the girls skipped back and forth. Dad said if you're a man, then nothing can hurt you. Dad said walk tall, don't crawl like some little nigger. But Tommytwo felt almost grateful to accept a jar of mayonnaise and carry it to the table. You're no man, you're just a little nigger, Tommytwo imagined his dad saying as he carried the maraschino cherries and the butter dish across the room and set them on the counter. Dad could talk, because Dad didn't have sisters.

It all happened so quickly. He should fit inside now, said Stormy, and Hilary caught him in a headlock. Then they closed the refrigerator door, poking at his fingers with a fork to keep him back. Tommytwo sat, terrified and humiliated, on a cold shelf. He sobbed, softly so Mom wouldn't come, and waited to die. He could hear his sisters laughing on the outside.

————

Mabel loved her family. Which was why this . . . hatred . . . she felt whenever she glanced Tom's way kept her short of breath and even queasy all afternoon and finally knocked her down into one of the straight-back chairs set in Ma's front room to accommodate the mourners. Mabel had married an uppity man.

She stared Tom down, disgusted, as he moved his eyes across the rickety cabinet Ma used to like to call her chifforobe and tried to hide his dimple inside a flurry of coughs. A man who nobody in this room could look at without seeing raggedy pants and a makeshift suitcase, laughing at the poverty of an old woman's home on the day of her funeral.

"Oh yes. Yes, of course. Boscoe." There he went again, pretending he didn't recognize the other mourners, not even Boscoe Brown, not even Old Man Apron Wilson. And he kept that spine straight, bone straight, as he refused plate after plate of Sister Mercy's fine greens and neckbones. People tried to pay that woman for her neckbones and greens, and here he was, turning it down as if it were fast food. Lips tracing numbers instead of participating in conversation—still thinking about the offers he'd been getting from fancy law firms after winning that arson case, no doubt. Dimple dancing at Ma's funeral, good God in heaven.

Folk used to warn her about Tom Spader. It was Boscoe Brown himself who'd pointed out years ago that nobody'd ever nicknamed that boy. Not the barber, not even the kids in his class. All that bright skin and clay-colored hair, Lord knew he was ripe for getting tagged Red. But he'd stayed Tom Spader, and kids and adults alike had sought out Mabel and told her to watch her step. Boy's trouble, boy ain't one of us.

Tom's nostrils suddenly flared when he glanced at Ma's lopsided wallpaper. Mabel knew exactly what he was thinking: Looked like some nigger high on heroin had hung that wallpaper. Let him laugh. Ma was a seventy-three-years-old arthritic widow when she hung it, and doing the best she could. Just trying to make something pretty out of this miserable shack. Negroes today had lost all their compassion.

"Mabel Agnes Turner. A sight for sore eyes."

Mabel stood and hugged somebody back. Someone ought to knock Tom Spader down a peg. Daddy would have done it. Daddy would have reminded Tom of the day he'd come to Lovejoy, dirty, disheveled, and violent. And now had the audacity to act like somebody *else* was the nigger. Never *saw* a negro so filthy and violent as Tom Spader that very first day. The woman was seventy-three when she hung that wallpaper, he ought to be applauding.

Whoever this man was still hugging Mabel, he certainly hadn't lingered too long in his morning shower. She frowned and took a whiff. Smelled like somebody she hadn't known too well, and might not have liked too much.

"Hello . . . ?" she finally said, and they must have known each other growing up, because he launched right into a discussion about how much the Lord had blessed him, although it looked to Mabel like all the Lord had done was stuck him in a cheap suit. Peasy hair seemed as though it had never seen a comb. Had the nerve to have on cuff links. Couldn't be Rawley Jones. No, she'd heard Rawley'd been killed in a scuffle.

Right off the bat, the fellow steered the conversation toward Africa, which more and more black fellows liked to do these days, no matter what the question. Lord but that got on Mabel's nerves. This one was going to buy an airplane and fly everybody back home to Africa. He was going to buy the fuel from the Libyans, because the Libyans understood the black man's plight. Mabel tried to say mm-hmmm in all the right places as she kept an eye on Tom in a chair across the room. She'd asked him not to wear those Bally shoes to Lovejoy; these old men's feet hurt bad enough without having to see that. Too cocky to even dull the shine.

Whoever this negro was all up in Mabel's face, he wasn't shy. He held a slide of Africa up to the sunlight through a tear in the curtain. Mabel said Oh my, although all it showed was some shirtless colored fellows crouched in the dirt drinking Coca-Cola, which she certainly didn't need to travel all the way back to Africa to see. She tried to spot Tom, but the chair he'd been sitting on was suddenly empty. The fellow cleared his throat and announced he was going to build his own air-control compound and tower. Because The Man would let a plane full of colored crash right into the ocean.

Big Brother was already out on the porch drinking beers and telling stories. Mabel wouldn't mind sneaking out of here early. But God Almighty, whoever this fellow was, he must think Mabel was his mother confessor. Now he was bragging about being incorporated, calling himself an entrepreneur. He was going to finance his airplane scheme by selling pork through mail order, apparently. Worked out of his home, which Mabel would guess by the smell of him was government housing. He pulled out a rubber band full of dog-eared business cards and handed one to Mabel. The calligraphy was so convoluted, she would have sworn his name was Poison.

"Pea Pie Persons!" shouted Old Man Apron Wilson from across the room at the very same instant, and Mabel felt like she'd been jabbed with an electrified prod. The imprint of Pea Pie's embrace turned into a tingling rash, and the air grew thick with his sour smell. "Pork got a future!" Old Man Apron cried, weaving closer on his cane, hearing-aid wires curling out of a breast pocket.

A single thought stung Mabel over and over: This moron could have been her husband. This barely washed negro was her daddy's first preference. She'd narrowly escaped a life-time of listening to this negro pontificate while she washed sheets to keep food on the table.

She tried to focus on the business card. "Albert 'Pea Pie' Persons: Pork Got a Future." Was he insane? The card was dirty, and dog-eared, and orange, and this was how he ran a business supposed to take the race home? Telephone number scratched out and a new one scrawled across the bottom in pencil? And her daddy would have walked her down the aisle to this man? For the first time since the undertaker had thrown the dirt on Ma's casket, Mabel felt a breakdown com-ing on. She clawed the wall to keep her balance as she rose up on tiptoe, desperate to spot her husband.

"You got my sign-up fee, Pea Pie. First of the month," Old Man Apron shouted past Mabel, breath as hot as a wood-burning oven.

"Pea Pie's bringing Jesus' blessings to Lovejoy," Sister

Mercy called out, and the curls on her blue wig shimmied as she clapped her hands. "A pyramid plan, just like on *Sixty Minutes*. Everybody in this room gonna be rich, rich, rich. Come on, Pea Pie, stand up here and learn us all about selling pork." Bosoms and hips pressed into Mabel, humidity plugged her sinuses. People came in from the porch and packed tighter and tighter into Ma's front room to hear talk about money. The only teenager present whistled through his fingers when Mercy said Pork, and the room took on a revival-meeting hush.

"Got to get into the System," said Pea Pie, and he was in his glory, boosting onto the leg of a rickety chair. "We gots to get All us black folk into the System," he said, voice rising for the whole room to hear. "Gots to get us the Means to get into the System," he said, shouting toward the mourners out in the kitchen. "Then take out some of what we put In to the System, and use it for our own Nay-shun-buil-ding!"

Lord in heaven, where in the world was Tom. Had he somehow left her here? Oh, thank God, there. There he was, there he was. All this humidity had blurred Mabel's vision. There he was, off in a corner, temple ticking, in one of his usual trances. Probably weighing options, planning which wall to knock down next. He'd told her he was going take his time choosing his next move, wait until he got an offer from one of the big firms with offices in Greenwich or Stamford. The Spaders' whole future glowed like a sunshiny day.

Across the room, he suddenly winked at her, lifting his chin ironically at Pea Pie on his makeshift pulpit, dimple dancing for one tiny instant. She smiled back, for Tom's eyes only, and she sighed with a sudden contentment.

————

Tommytwo hated his new karate class. His butt was about to get beat, right on the mat, while the whole class watched. Word was out, Chuckie was going to crunch him so bad he'd start speaking in tongues like Lola Morales's bald-headed grandmomma. His ass would be grass. White Ralph broke the news to Tommytwo, including the part about Chuckie having brought his brother's fighting shoes to finish Tommytwo off in the parking lot afterward. Tommytwo knew he was telling the truth because the four girls in the class kept coning their hands around each other's ears to tell secrets, and pointing at him.

While the girls sparred, Tommytwo asked three separate guys if they wanted to come over to his house after class and play Battleship. Even White Ralph said no. Tommytwo felt sick to his guts. Ball Odell, whose parents forced him to take karate because he got his butt beat almost every day, weasled up to him while the last Puerto Rican girl was getting massacred on the mat. Ball said, Keep your dick cupped.

Stand tall like a man, don't crawl like a nigger, Tommytwo chanted inside his head as he slunk out to the middle of the mat, where Chuckie already stood, laughing like a murderous fiend. Tommytwo held on to his dick, waiting. Mr. Siegel, the coach, blew his whistle. Right then, a miracle happened. Outside the window, Tommytwo's mom appeared in the parking lot, in her yellow ladybug dress. Tommytwo loosened his hands from his nuts and pointed. Kids started looking toward the window. There was his dad, too, standing right beside his mom. Tommy bounded off the mat and waved out the window. When Dad saw Tommytwo, he yelled out, Hey there, son, how about it?

And then Tommytwo saw it, a brand-new car! It was beautiful, oh man, oh man, so beautiful he couldn't believe it. Silver like a race car. His sisters looked great too, bouncing inside the window, so high their heads banged against the ceiling and they screamed with silent laughter. Tommy Spader's got a VOLVO? said Chuckie, scratching his dumb carrot-top head.

Tommytwo walked right past Chuckie, then past Lola Morales. She stuck her tongue out at him, but in a way like maybe he should try saying hi to her next time. Past Mr. Siegel, who clapped Tommytwo on the back like they were best friends, even though everybody knew Mr. Siegel hated kids. Still wanna play Battleship? said White Ralph. Nope, said Tommytwo, feeling ten feet tall. Maybe in your next life.

1978

GREENWICH
MEAN TIME

Mabel wasn't raised in a barn, so it was only natural to say hello to a woman walking dog and children. They were going to be neighbors, after all, once she got all these boxes moved inside. The woman had one of these white-lady afros, all full of spray, and she seemed timid. She stopped short at Mabel's hello and stared, eyebrows up to her hairline.

Mabel wished she'd gone heavier on the deodorant this morning; there were two big circles of dried sweat on her shirt. The woman stared at Mabel's hand before she shook it, looking as if Mabel were offering a plate of stale cookies. They stood there in the most awkward silence Mabel had ever been a party to, watching the movers tramp boxes up and down the truck's ramp like show dogs.

I'm Mrs. Bonner, the woman finally said. I live in the yellow house catty-corner. I'm Mrs. Spader, Mabel replied, and the woman blinked, as if Mabel had shot a dart. Which was when Mabel began to wonder if the woman was one of these schizophrenic, split-personality types. She glanced down at the woman's children, who were all done up like packages of candy with all sorts of ribbons and bows, fat little hands peeling back mama's skirt to cover their eyes. They seemed normal enough.

You must be praying, the woman blurted out, and Mabel just stood there on the curb, arms dangling at her side, wondering what in the world that comment meant. Back when Luisa Rodriguez moved to Hamden, Mabel had carried over a pineapple upside-down cake and listened to Luisa talk Spanish for over two hours, nodding her head the whole while. Someone could argue that that encounter was just as bizarre a beginning for two neighbors as this one. And she and Luisa had gone on to be friends.

You must be praying that they won't break the lamps, Mrs. Bonner said, eyes no bigger than specks of pepper, blinking at Mabel. Mabel smiled and listened and tried to understand, just as she'd done with Luisa.

"They've put you in charge out here, so you must be praying the movers don't break these gorgeous lamps and get you in trouble." The woman sounded out the words one by one, as if Mabel were the one losing her mind. Those movers better not break Mabel's lamps, not unless they felt like losing money. Mabel would be first in line at that bank, canceling the check tomorrow morning if she found anything broken. She kept on smiling.

"So . . . when do they arrive?" said the woman, pointing past Mabel at the Spaders' new house.

"Who?" Mabel took her own peek backward.

"Them. The new family."

"Uh, they're already in there," said Mabel, and by now she was talking dubiously out of the side of her own face. "Unpacking boxes."

"Wonderful! Tell them Anne Marie Bonner down the street said she just can't wait to meet them," said the woman, just as the puppy broke loose from his leash. Mabel wished she had a dog biscuit to throw it as a thank you; this bizarre conversation was making her dizzy. The woman took her girls and trotted away with a cheery shrug and no good-bye. Mabel just stared after them. Greenwich, Connecticut. Yes indeed.

———

Stormy, who generally stayed home and wrote poetry, was so delighted over never having to do the dishes or clean her room anymore that early one morning she was inspired to write a poem called "Sylvia Falcon: Maid Extraordinaire." After the kids left for school and her mom for the mall, she transferred it onto a piece of stationery, using really beautiful handwriting, and gave it to Sylvia Falcon, who leaned on her mop and snorted the whole time she was reading it and then turned to Stormy and flat out told her: "Girl, ya'll mama must be insane. Raising ya'll out here around nothing but crackers. 'Worth my weight in gold.' You even sound like one of them. Wouldn't mind a self-made brother myself, but not to set me up in some lily-white suburb. White folk'll get half a notion and burn you out your home. I'm telling you."

And from that morning on, Sylvia more or less never

stopped talking. She talked about everybody and everything. Sylvia wanted to get married when she was twenty-eight, which was in a year and seventy days, but not to her current boyfriend, because he liked to sit home too much. She was a Leo, and she drank all the tomato juice she could get her hands on because it cured a spotty complexion, and she was trying to come up with some way to wear her hair without chemicals, but still cute.

In the mornings if Mom was busy getting the kids off, Sylvia would carry the tray of tea and Cap'n Crunch with fruit into Stormy, and help her with her coughing fits: Sylvia's chin lifted meant "Make more of a wet, snot sound" and her nostrils rounded out meant "Girl, tone down the drama before I bust out laughing." And that was pretty much how Stormy and Sylvia became friends. Best friends.

Then one day their friendship fell into jeopardy. Stormy was taking a week off school due to an outbreak of scabies, whose telltale rash could be made with a fork chilled in the back of the freezer overnight. After Mom and Dad and the kids left, she slid down the banister to where Sylvia was waxing the front hallway floor, and she hung there upside down. Sylvia saw her hanging there by her knees but she didn't say good morning. It was obvious she had not been having a very good day so far. Stormy scooted closer down the banister, arms bumping each balustrade. Sylvia finally let her hear what she was thinking.

"Who that man think he is. Would have thought I asked for gold bullion and not a five-dollar raise. Never seen a brother turn so cold. Something's wrong with that brother. Something wrong with your daddy, child."

Sylvia kept muttering, but Stormy couldn't keep listening because hearing even that much made her sick inside. Sylvia shouldn't be saying those things about her daddy. Her head hurt from hanging upside down and her nose was getting clogged and she was suddenly crying and it was all so embarrassing that Stormy for some reason shouted, "My daddy's perfectly normal!" which was such an obvious lie that Sylvia set down the blue mop and planted her wrist on her hip. And she said nothing, she merely looked Stormy up and down, and Stormy could feel the disgust. Breath drawn sharply in, then whistled out down the other end of the hall, as if Sylvia couldn't even stand to look at her anymore.

"I see," Sylvia finally said, lightly yet decisively, "you know it's true but you choose to front." And Stormy had a sudden flash of lying alone in her bed, watching dumb cartoons day after day, eating Mom's bologna-and-cheese sandwiches.

So she said, "Wait! I have something to tell you," and she found herself telling the one story she'd never even written in her journal. The story about the legal pad.

"What legal pad," Sylvia said dismissively, tilting wax to the sides of the bucket and dipping the mop in.

And Stormy told how she'd taken the key to Dad's office from his penny jar in the dressing room and gone looking for fancy stationery to write a letter to Charlie's Angels. And she'd sat in Dad's chair and that's when she'd seen it, the legal pad, and she started to tear off a sheet when she saw a page filled with markings . . .

"What kind of 'markings'?" said Sylvia.

"Shh," Stormy said, because she'd almost forgot to mention the page was six sheets down from the front of the pad, six empty sheets. Which was the crucial part of the story. It almost seemed as though the page was purposefully hidden, particularly since the blank pages above it had not been creased back.

"Something he wrote down?" said Sylvia, fingertips rubbing down her throat.

Her dad had used number-three pencil and drawn an entire tapestry, full of curls and turrets. So light that Stormy could barely even make out the words in the center . . .

"What words?" said Sylvia, flinching.

" 'Always remember they're watching us,' " whispered Stormy, and Sylvia shuddered like crazy and said Noooo.

"That's why your behind ought to be in school. Learning something useful. Daddy probably end up in the insane asylum." Sylvia threatened, but she looked pleased with the information, and Stormy could see the friendship was back on track again. She lobbed a comfortable old complaint to clinch the deal.

"A kid called me a monkey the last time I went to school!"

"So? He white? Well, then call his mama a white baboon, stop him right in his tracks. Girl, just grit your teeth and go. It's only the seventh grade. Run get my box of beads. Let's at least try and braid this stuff while we watch our story. Mama left you up in here looking like a banshee."

Stormy galloped up the stairs. Sylvia was going to give her teeny-tiny flippable braids—wonderful. And she had three more days' worth of scabies. And today on *All My Kids,* Erica Kane's husband Tom was going to discover she was still sneaking birth-control pills. Life was perfect.

She stopped skipping as she rounded the corner past Tommytwo's bedroom. She tapped the linen-closet door, clinging closely to the wall. She hated to go past Daddy's office at the end of the hall. "Prevent Whiteflight," that's what had really been in the middle of that tapestry, painstakingly woven in to be almost invisible. She was never going to let anyone know how weird her dad was. Her dad was really weird.

———

Mabel snuggled deep into her bed, legs scrunched to her chest, feet balled, body wound so tight her spine got plucked every time Hilary brushed against her. Hilary had been going through a sleep-with-mama phase ever since they moved to Greenwich. Mabel wasn't going to let it go on much longer.

The truth was, Mabel was having a hard time adjusting to Greenwich herself. As pretty as this town looked, she felt like she was walking on pins and needles. When she tried to put her finger on why, all she could think about was the missing sidewalks. Whoever was in charge had forgotten to lay sidewalks. The neighborhood was as quiet as a ghost town. It was a miracle if she ever saw somebody milling about outside to say hello to.

And don't let anybody tell the lie that white folk don't beat on one another, that only the niggers did that. The Bonners in the yellow house catty-corner doused cold water right on that theory. Had two little girls same grade as Tommytwo, the Bonner girls. The woman came to PTA but sat in the back of the auditorium. Always trying to coerce that teaspoon of hair into a natural, never did come by and say that big hello she'd promised. Days that man was going to beat her, his neck would be a tight red column as he bent to pick up his newspaper. Mabel'd watched him from her window this very afternoon. Whole head redder than a stop sign.

Tom was twisting in the sheets and kicking; he always slept like he was fighting World War Three. He calmed right down when Mabel started reaching over him for the telephone to have beside her in case she finally had to call the police on those people tonight.

"Careful, careful. Mabel. Careful, don't. Careful. Careful." His eyes were still closed but she knew he'd be wide awake in a minute, period, unless she put the phone down. Last thing she felt like hearing was a lecture on fitting in, which would start with the Bonners but could cruise all the way around to keeping her Millie Jackson albums in the back of the stack and even touch on the *Jet* magazine before he got tired of talking. Mabel put the phone down. Tom did have a point.

All she truly wanted was to get a good night's sleep and then get up tomorrow morning and get her husband and children baconed and egged and out to school and off to work. Peace, that was all she'd ever wanted, and a happy home life for her family. Only colored woman in town not cleaning houses, she'd be a fool to start spouting off about how things ought to run, she knew that. Her best bet was to keep her two cents to herself, and just be thankful they'd made it to Greenwich at all.

The first shriek out of the catty-corner house felt like a gunshot in Mabel's stomach. Her neck bucked out from the pillow. She repeated to herself what Lola, who cleaned for the Bonners, had told Sylvia Falcon, who'd told Mabel: The woman asked for it, plain and simple. The one time the police had showed up, it was Anne Marie Bonner herself who had sent them away.

Mabel put a hand on her chest to calm her heartbeat rate back down. Calm down, Mabel Agnes, she told herself, it'll be sunny in the morning. She tried flipping over onto her stomach. No peace there. She tried her side. Nothing.

Thank goodness for small favors, the children never said a word about Mrs. Bonner getting beaten, probably thought it was alleycats in heat. The only one who brought the subject up regularly was Mabel's live-in housekeeper, Sylvia Falcon.

"Mmmmm," she greeted Mabel on mornings after, skittering that hum up several octaves to reveal, in language Mabel understood perfectly, that she still could not believe white folks—and rich ones at that—beat on each other so bad. That mmm was the first note in what normally grew to a whole conversation, with a pot of coffee set on the table and a bowl of ice fetched, and a carton of cream stuck down in it.

Black and blue. And that ain't no random expression, Sylvia told Mabel, scooting her chair in closer. The whole left side of that woman's face looked like somebody'd rammed into it with a telephone pole out by the mailbox early this morning. Big-ass bruise up the whole side of her face, gray and blue and black and even some orange. Yes, ma'am, some man put his hands on Sylvia Falcon, she'd show him what for, said Sylvia. Mabel ought to be down on her knees thanking Jesus for sending her a man as good as Mr. Spader to provide for her and treat her right.

"Did she catch you taking a peek?" said Mabel.

Sylvia's big egg-shaped eyes batted, stayed shut tight for emphasis as she cleared her throat like a car motor.

"I coughed, that loud."

"What'd she do?"

"She played blind—"

"Oooh, I hate that. The other day I walked into a boutique and not one salesgirl—"

"Let me finish telling my story, Miz Spader, because you are not going to believe—"

"Go on."

"Clapped her hand to the side of her face"—Sylvia did her imitation—"and called out My tooth! My tooth! and ran back in the house. Toothache, my black behind."

"That situation's a crime shame. By the way, did this week's *Jet* come?"

At first Mabel had felt funny hiring somebody black to clean her house, but Tom had been firm about not rocking that particular boat. Hire someone black, he'd told her, dropping a good-bye kiss on her cheek, then smoothing the spot with his thumb. Black black.

It turned out Mabel enjoyed having Sylvia around. She reminded Mabel just the slightest bit of Ma. Ma used to race Mrs. Bledsoe next door to hang the sheets out to dry, clothespins popping out of the box. Sylvia was the same way, making the beds so fast she was a blur, if it was getting anywhere near time for her story.

And Sylvia understood not to ask questions about certain family customs. For instance, Tom's new custom of not permitting *Jet* magazine in the house, let alone having it delivered; no need to scare the mailman, according to Tom. Poor slob might start thinking they were separtists. So week after week, Sylvia kept each issue hidden for Mabel until morning coffee, patting her smock pockets to signal she was keeping a secret. Mabel hoped Sylvia and the girls realized, when their time came, that a woman was right to keep some things to herself. As far as Mabel was concerned, hiding her subscription to *Jet* was no bigger a deal than a couple of plucked-out chin hairs. No reason for a man to know all a woman's business.

"Wait, child, turn the page back. Look at that kidney-shaped swimming pool. A four-THOUsand-dollar swimming pool on a full acre of land in upstate New York, good Lord in heaven. John Amos . . . who is that? John Amos . . . That name is so familiar . . ."

"Used to play the daddy on *Good Times*. Keep turning,

they got a picture of Esther Rolle's ranch. Half a million dollars, six bathrooms. Ya'll just two bathrooms back."

"Don't forget our half-bath down in the basement."

"That's right! Appreciate it, girl. He doin' you right."

Mabel rolled her eyes, pleased.

"Seven dollars for that little bitty box of cookies he brought you home." Sylvia arched her eyebrow at Mabel. "I saw that price tag."

Mabel sniffed to keep from smiling. "We'll see if they taste like seven dollars' worth later on. I'll save you one. Today's the day."

"Your PTA group?"

"This afternoon, unless they postpone again."

"We need eggs if you want me to fix my pound cake."

"You think those ladies drink root beer?" Mabel frowned toward Sylvia, who scrunched her nose back at Mabel.

"Let me call Haiwatha. Woman she work for come from money."

"The good glasses clean?"

"Should be. That bad Freddy Hurd mama coming?"

"Said she was."

"Tell her that boy need his butt whipped into a holy frenzy."

Mabel raised an eyebrow at Sylvia, who snorted. No need to even say it. Only a bigger fool than Mabel would try telling Mrs. Hurd that rotten brat of hers needed a whipping. Hey, Miz Spader, coons got tails? he'd shouted at Mabel just the other day, then sped away on a shiny new three-speed bike.

"I wish I would. You heard from your mama lately? How's her bursitis?"

"Still swearing by onion till the day she dies. Says it cools the burning. Pour you another cup of coffee?"

"Just one more."

Sylvia poured the last of the pot into their cups and chopped at the sugar stuck to the bottom of the bowl. "Lou Ella sang the solo at yesterday's service. Girl got a voice could beat Aretha."

"I saw her standing out there at the bus stop last Friday. Said the pastor asked her special."

"Mm-hmm. The whole place was rocking. Come on go with us next Sunday."

Mabel stirred sugar into her coffee, then added cream drop by drop. "We'll see."

"Plenty of room in the Pontiac with me and Lou Ella and Nay-Nay."

"Nay-Nay's the one with the blow hair, works for the Hurds?"

"Mm-hmm. She drives on Sunday mornings. Plenty of room in her Pontiac. And had her brother to fix the heat."

Mabel knew just what dress she'd wear if she went to church, her purple silk with feathers up the side from Bloomingdale's. It was still in the plastic up in Mabel's closet. The salesgirl had shown her how to wrap the shawl a certain way she'd brought back from Atlanta. Mabel could just see herself stepping up into that church in her sharp dress. Her touch-up was just two weeks old so she could wear the matching hat and leave her neck bare if she chose.

She also knew just what Tom would say if he saw her getting into a Pontiac with Sylvia and Nay-Nay and the rest of the local maids, even on a Sunday morning. And they'd probably honk the horn and wake the whole neighborhood, to boot. Sylvia had quit stirring her coffee and was tapping her spoon handle on the *Jet,* staring at Mabel with eyes as sharp as an eagle's. Maybe Mabel could arrange to meet the girls someplace near the church . . . Sylvia was watching her so hard she made Mabel slosh her coffee.

"We'll see how the week goes," said Mabel, trying to sound offhand. "I've got all this mess I need to take care of . . ."

"Fine," muttered Sylvia, long forehead shoved up into all the wrinkles it could hold. She wiped off the carton of cream and pulled open the refrigerator door.

Don't forget to tell Mother Hubbard Hurd I said that boy needs his ass whipped, Sylvia said, sliding downstairs in her house slippers as the first car rolled up to the curb. Mabel looked at her watch—five minutes early. She could sense her hypertension.

It was Tom that turned this PTA meeting into an event. He'd started out teasing her late last week. Best serve these seven-dollar cookies, best say "potahto" and "tomahto." That man, in a good mood all week over favorable rulings in the commuter-vigilante case he was trying, had everyone from Tommy on up to Sylvia in a state of tender funnybone. The kids were sticking their pinkies out when they drank their Nestlé Quik, and not even Mabel could keep from laughing while Sylvia wiped the spilt milk.

Then Tom came home somber and quiet last night, looking as though he'd seen a ghost. He told her he'd heard news down at the office she needed to be aware of. Closed the bedroom door and talked slow and loud as if she were deaf. It's a Big Deal they agreed to hold this PTA meeting at our house, he told her, and she noticed a new red vein threaded through the white of his eye. It seems they've made an Exception, it seems someone has taken a Liking to you, doesn't want you to feel bad even though what you did at that PTA meeting Is Not Done. Not By New People.

Mabel waited for him to explain why a bunch of mothers planning a school Halloween party had to be a surgical procedure, but he launched off on a tangent instead. Tell John Lindo's wife, Kathy, about that gardenia garden your mother used to have back in St. Louis. I know, Mabel, I know, but Say gardenia, all right? What's the Point if you've got to say cabbage? What's the point of any of this, Mabel? We're well on our way, That's the point. Isn't it, sweetheart?

The way Mabel saw it, it had only been natural to offer to hostess the meeting to plan the Halloween party. Of course, that was way back before it would have ever crossed Mabel's mind that a meeting to decide who'd be xeroxing flyers and hanging streamers might have to follow some fancy protocol.

It was also back before old Lana Turner next door started surveilling her monkey-looking dog through her screen whenever she put it out to urinate, as if Mabel or one of her children was harboring an inclination to run out there and snatch it up. Mabel was sick of these white women around here. Smarmy by day, screechy by night.

These PTA ladies would get their one chance to tango with Mabel, and that was all. They liked her. The nerve of those women. They were coming to Mabel's house, Mabel's five-bedroom, five-bathroom verge-of-a-mansion. Those women better hope she liked them. Take away the white and the rich and it was only a bunch of children's mamas coming to plan the Halloween dance, Mabel told herself in her foyer, tapping her toe as she waited for them to ring the bell before she opened the door.

"Mrs. Spader."

"Mrs. Hurd."

"Mrs. Spader!"

"Hello, Mrs. Rainier."

Becka reminded us where we'd met you before, one of the ladies greeted Mabel. Yes, thanks to Becka for reminding us, echoed somebody else. The Bar Association banquets. With that husband, that impressive Tom Spader. That charming man, added in a redhead with a big behind hidden badly beneath a clinging caftan she shouldn't have been trying to wear in the first place. Welcome, someone else said, handing Mabel a plant tied with satin ribbons.

Becka Rainier—It's Rahn-yay, but don't you worry, Mabel, nobody gets it right the first time—winked at Mabel like a secret lover. Moments later, Mabel found herself strolling arm-in-arm with the woman down the hallway toward the living room. Becka was beaming at her with flared nostrils. "Ggrrr!" she growled at Mabel when they finally reached the living room, apparently just that happy. Mabel grinned back, big, although she'd missed the punch line.

PTA meetings hadn't run this way in Hamden. At this one, there were a whole lot more pantyhose and fancy purses than Mabel had expected. They had a special secretary who read a progress report about hayrides and ponyrides at somebody's father's ranch. Nobody said a word about strewing confetti around the school lunchroom, which Mabel might have known something about. Mabel sat quiet, wishing she'd splurged on another couple boxes of seven-dollar cookies rather than setting regular old honey-roast peanuts around in the canister. The secretary took notes in a leather notebook. Real leather.

The meeting stuck to a strict agenda, although Helen Hurd took time to salt and pepper each item with stories about her nasty-mouthed Freddy. Mabel ahhed and awwed, feeling uneasy. Becka's warm smiles suddenly glowing at her every few minutes only underlined the fact that Mabel didn't have a friend in the world. Tina Johnson was always promising to drive out and spend the weekend, but no telling when that would be, now that she'd gone and let Charlie, with all his kingdoms in ancient Egypt and no health insurance, impregnate her again.

Mabel was so busy feeling sorry for herself that the smell of sweaty nylons caught her off guard. The women were starting to toe off their shoes and get comfortable. There was some sort of game being played, right in the meeting. Mabel perked up in her seat.

The rules seemed to be, each time Helen Hurd bragged about her Freddy, Becka Rainier—Rahn-yay, if you please—rolled those round blue eyes. Rolled them so hard they just about rolled right off the edge of that narrow oval head. White woman knew how to roll herself some eyeball, yes, she most certainly did.

"And then Freddy said, But Mummy!" Helen Hurd would say, and Becka Rainier would set those pupils spinning like pinballs. Others were in on it too, pitching their own eyeballs like marbles, two and three sets erupting simultaneously. Mabel had to fight to keep a straight face.

Well, thank goodness. She'd known there had to be some crazy girls in this tired town to have some fun with. She almost wished her daughters could be here to witness this, especially Hilary. Little Miss Blue Jeans was convinced the fun had to end if you stepped into a dress. But this Rahn-yay woman was the perfect lady. Had herself on skin shoes with matching handbag, hair spray, nylons, the whole bit. And having herself a grand old time, eyeballs shooting around curves ninety miles an hour.

"And guess who's volunteered to carve the Great Pumpkin?" Helen Hurd sang out, dimples nearly pinched into two pieces.

"Freddy," coughed somebody down at the other end of the sofa, and Mrs. Hurd kept right on yapping. Something about all these white ladies in their hair spray acting up like teenage girls tickled Mabel terribly. She nearly laughed right out, but managed to cover it up with a sneeze. Which was when Becka Rainer swooped in on Mabel with those pinball eyes. And before Mabel could say boo, there she was, drawn into the game.

"Did I share what Freddy said this morning while Nay-Nay was pouring him his Cocoa Puffs?"

Becka Rainier egged Mabel on from across the room, somehow got her to send a loop-de-loop over to Mrs. Hathaway, who was perched on the little antique chair Tom had insisted on buying, despite it being as hard as a cast-iron pot.

"He said, and this was a classic, 'Mummy, if we dropped Nay-Nay into a giant bowl of milk . . .' " Hazel-green eyes ping-ponged at Mabel from Kathy Lindo, that redhead woman who put the *b* in "big behind." Mabel was too busy concentrating on shooting an under-the-eyelid roll over to the Horchison grandmother to notice Helen Hurd was done telling Freddy stories. She was shuffling papers together, telling the secretary to xerox the minutes. Too late, though, now Becka Rainier and all the rest of them were playful as a litter of puppies, which didn't bother Mabel one bit. She didn't have any more tea biscuits but there were plenty more oranges and iced tea if some people wanted to stay around afterward and shoot some breeze. Mabel reminded herself to ask Becka Rahn-yay where in the world she'd found those pretty skin shoes.

"Uh-oh!" that fool Becka was screeching now, neck arched and arm feeling down to the floor, probably fixing to make a game out of some stubborn clump of fluff from underneath the sofa. Let me walk this woman to the door before things get too silly, thought Mabel, rising as Helen Hurd snapped her purse closed and wiggled her pink-tipped fingers goodbye. Except Helen had stopped in her tracks and was opening her purse back up and feeling around for her glasses. Mabel's whole hundred and fifty-some pounds jammed deep into the toes of her shoes as she glanced over at Becka Rainier and realized what had snagged all the ladies' attention.

That damn *Jet* magazine. It must have slipped out of Sylvia's smock pocket while she was unzipping the plastic sofa cover this morning. My Doris buys that rag, somebody called out. I've seen it at my house, somebody else chimed in. Becka Rainier was pawing through the glossy pages as if she'd found gold. Mabel should have canceled that subscription months back, like Tom told her to. Coulda woulda shoulda. Lord, Lord, Lord.

And now Becka Rainer's knees were knocking together to make room for more ladies on the sofa, nylon hose shooting out sparks from the friction. Redhead woman with the big rear end was so excited she twisted her skirt trying to scoot in closer. Mabel could feel all those manicured fingertips pointing the same as if they were picking at the skin across her bosom. She shuddered and Becka Rainier gave her a big wink from across the coffee table.

"Have they no pride," sighed Helen Hurd while the rest of the ladies guffawed at Miss October's macramé swimsuit. Mabel should have canceled that damn subscription before they'd ever moved to Greenwich, but no, she'd sent in a change-of-address form instead. Too smart for her own good. Mortified in her own living room, that's where it ended her up, wishing she could sink into the hardwood floorboards. Her pinkie finger drew itself out straight as a chicken bone as she pretended to sip her tea.

Becka Rainier conjured up a Southern accent to read aloud. Television Stahs Lib Duh Good Laf, she drawled, and the rest of them fell over one another, choking with laughter. What kind of magazine calls someone a celebrity that nobody on the entire planet has ever even heard of, somebody said. A kidney-shaped pool, that's not news! someone else cried out.

Don't you never, never trust 'em, folks with sense used to say about white folk. And here was Mabel, living so close to them the air in her house smelled like wet chickens if she kept the windows open on rainy days—the old wives' tale was more than a notion. Esther Rolle was the smart one, found a ranch in the country, away from all this nonsense. Mabel's children would be banging open the door any minute. She'd tell these ladies the meeting had come to a close, and she'd put a sharp enough edge on it that they'd understand exactly what she meant.

"What a waste of money," sniffed Helen Hurd. "Poor suckers." Old big-behind Kathy Lindo practically shook her head loose from her neck agreeing, but Becka Rainier couldn't let the subject drop. Put her hand on her hip and rolled those blue eyes, out in the open this time, for everyone to see. Stirring up trouble, that was all that woman was good for. White women thought the whole world was a violin primed for them to pluck. Mabel reminded herself to open the windows and air this place out the minute they left.

"Seventy-five cents won't break them," Becka Rainier told Helen Hurd. "They work hard enough for their money, they can decide how to spend it."

"Some prudence wouldn't hurt them," Helen Hurd snapped

back. "No telling where they'd be if they started saving a portion of their pay each week." Fourteen necks, including Mabel's, cracked as they pivoted back to Becka.

"You know, Helen, I'd like to get you down on your hands and knees and scrub somebody's floors the way my Callie does before you try telling those women how to spend their money."

Somebody sucked her breath in, and necks cracked back to Helen, all except Mabel's. It was starting to sink in that nobody had seen the name Mrs. Mabel Spader on the mailing label on the back of the *Jet*. As far as they were concerned, whoever had shined the hardwood floors had bought this *Jet* magazine. Mabel was poised to tell the women that yes, somebody on this planet did so know John Amos. He was the father on *Good Times,* thank you very, very much. But at the same time, the tension was falling out of her shoulders like apples dropping off a tree.

Tom Spader appeared in Mabel's mind just then, eyes bloodshot, back slumped over the futility of it all. She was on the verge of throwing all his hard work down the drain. "Commuter-vigilante," that was my doing, he'd bragged all week about the phrase he'd coined to make his newest client more like a hero and less like a killer who'd shot a street-person point-blank in the face. Hell, yes, I'm a genius! he'd said back to the eleven o'clock news when the anchorman used his phrase. I even spelled the word out for those dumb-cluck reporters, he said, awestruck, every time news cameras panned across lines of irate suburbanites in Greenwich and Stamford demanding the shooter be bailed out on his own recognizance; she'd seen them herself, picket signs announcing that the windshield-smearing bums who preyed on home-bound commuters in the Merritt Parkway toll lines had finally got their just rewards. Yes, here her husband was, working himself sick to show white folk how smart a black man could be. And meanwhile, the first PTA meeting Mabel hostessed, every last ounce of negro inside her was threatening to bubble to the surface.

"Well, now, aren't we the admirable liberal, Becka Rainier. I'm leaving." Helen Hurd sniffed and clicked out to the hallway. Left all the rest of the ladies sitting there, blinking and talking about I Never.

"Tightass," whispered Becka, lighting a cigarette. Big-behinded Kathy Lindo was sniffling and wiping her eyes and a person could about choke on the ugly feelings floating through the air. Some situations turned into folklore unless you canceled them out before they ever really got started. Best way to do that was have somebody apologize. Apologies didn't cost a dime, made everyone feel good. So Mabel bit her tongue and went and got Miss Big Hiney a tissue and came back and apologized all around. Then stuttered through her bit about Ma's gardenias. Seemed like a lifetime before the rest of the women finally left, although it was probably no more than ten minutes.

———

Better keep out of Sylvia's way if she missed her *As the World Turns,* that had somehow become as much a house rule as no wet towels on beds. Mabel sighed as she carried the ladies' glasses to the kitchen and ran a sinkful of suds.

Seemed like everybody had their own little way of running things around this house. Seemed like everyone but Mabel got to stick their two cents in. She stuck her arms in the sink to the elbows, not noticing she'd run ice-cold water.

She'd always washed her gold-rimmed glasses by hand. Handled them like china dolls. Mabel washed the last glass and was about to rinse it when she suddenly blew the bubbles away from its rim and held it up to the light and saw as clear as writing what a fool she was. The gold rims on her glasses were nothing but a web of flakes and scratches. And what did she expect, she'd bought them at the Hamden Stop & Shop. Those PTA ladies were probably someplace having a ball, laughing themselves silly over Mabel's cheap glasses.

She plunged the glass back underwater and rubbed the rim hard. She fished a scouring pad out of the box beneath the sink and scrubbed until all the gold chipped off, scrubbed so viciously that she scraped a finger. Tears heated behind her eyes and she brought her hand up to suck. First thing tomorrow she was going out to the mall and buying crystal. Baccarat.

"Sylvia!" Mabel banged a fist on the counter. She had no business in here washing dishes herself, not with the amount of money she paid that woman. "Sylvia!"

Sylvia knocked open the swinging door, eyes darting from window to wall for intruders, as if Mabel surely would not be interrupting *As the World Turns* for anything less than armed robbery. And reeked of pepper from her daily tomato-juice cocktail. That ritual was over, Sylvia stretched out down there every day like a queen watching her story.

"You can leave the plastic cover off the sofa permanently," Mabel said. "Wrap the rest of the cheese."

Mabel wiped the soapsuds off her hands with a dishcloth and marched out of the kitchen. And that woman better ask somebody's permission the next time she went putting all those braids and beads in Stormy's hair. Had that child looking like some kind of banshee.

———

Hilary gazed out the classroom window. Yellow Monkeytown Express bus pulls into lot. Monkey bus goes over speed bump. Must be nine minutes to three. That dumb maid was probably letting Stormy paint her fingernails about now. Mr. Dunn droned on and on about who got what after World War Two. Like anybody cared. Monkey bus burps, like a big fat Chink, door farts open, driver steps out. Seven more minutes until three.

The monkey show was about to start. Soon there'd be one then two then twenty then thirty monkeys out there, scrabbling across the clean white entryway toward their bus. Teachers with a monkey in their class often let them leave early to catch the monkey bus, which gave the monkeys another unfair advantage besides the free lunch cards. Here came a couple of monkeys, shoving and shouting in their sub-English. Hilary wished the monkeys had never been invited to attend their school. They must have schools they could go to in their Monkeytown slum, wherever it was.

Chet Bank's father had a monkey man working in his piano shop who he trusted enough to give a key to the register, but these monkeys at this school didn't even lift a finger to earn anyone's trust. They slunk around like baboons and segregated themselves in the lunchroom. A lot of their parents were on welfare. The worst part was, their eyes watched you all the time.

Hilary casually scratched her forehead and let her hand drift upward and wipe. Mom hadn't had the energy for Hair Day this week, so Hilary'd had to resort to Vaseline to keep her cotton-candy hairline tame, and it dripped. Yesterday when Mr. Dunn got called out of the room Dana Peabody climbed on her desk and said what has six legs and says Ho Dee Doe, Ho Dee Doe and the answer was three niggers running for the elevator and Hilary had sat straight and tall like an Indian and let her lips drift into the cool smile and then the lookout kid had yelled He's Coming, and it had ended thank God it had ended.

"Penny for your thoughts." Mr. Dunn was beside her, whispering in her ear. Hilary smiled politely. What? He wanted to give her a penny for her thoughts? Oh crud, what was that stuff about Nuremberg? He waited, and his blue eyes crinkled like Santa Claus, and Hilary sat straight like an Indian, hating him, wondering why the heck she had to be his stupid teacher's pet. And wondering why white people got the good eyes and the good hair and the good everything.

"No thoughts," mumbled Hilary, shrinking away. The final bell rang. Another monkey dove for the bus, arms spiraling like propellers. Kami Murphy, who sat by the back window, snickered and Hilary knew why. Dumb monkey looked like he was being chased by a ghost.

"I certainly hope all that talking you engaged in earlier was well worth the twenty minutes' detention we will now embark upon." Mr. Dunn smiled at the class, waiting for someone to complain, because even one complaint meant ten extra minutes. Chet sat in the back cussing but Mr. Dunn couldn't hear him. Otherwise it was absolutely silent in the classroom. Dana Peabody glared around at people to keep the quiet so she could get to her baton club meeting on time. You could hear the Monkeytown Express revving up its engine outside. The bulk of the monkeys were now on board.

Mr. Dunn scanned the class for talkers. And that's when the nightmare began. He looked at Hilary, then looked away, then blinked, remembering something. She watched his every move. She watched him glance out the window at the Monkeytown Express, which was now closing its doors. Hilary fidgeted in her seat. It was as if she were watching herself getting blown off the edge of a cliff. The class sat in a stony silence. Mr. Dunn practically shouted his news.

"Hilary, you may go ahead and"—Hilary watched the words fall out of his mouth in excruciatingly slow motion— "catch your BUSSSS."

Hilary managed to time it so that she shouted "No thank you!"—the only thing that came to mind—at the exact same instant Mr. Dunn said "bus." Nothing happened next. Maybe, Hilary thought, maybe they hadn't heard him. Maybe they still believed she was an Indian ... seemed like maybe they still hadn't noticed she had to plaster her nappy ...

But how could Mr. Dunn think she was a monkey? Hadn't he ever seen her milling around, no hurry, every day after school like the rest of the kids, after all this time? Was he such an idiot that he had never even noticed that she *walked* home from school just like everybody else? Dana Peabody shifted around in her seat to look at Hilary. Dana's grimace was startling. It said, "I've been sitting in front of a gross monkey all this time and didn't even know it."

Stormy had jinxed her! This very morning, in the bathroom while Hilary was plastering down her edges with the Vaseline, Stormy'd circled her like a jackal and whispered, You're gonna hang. Then Stormy erupted in one of her fake cascades of sneezes and jumped back into bed.

Hilary swallowed dryly as she watched the bus pull out of the school lot. Dana Peabody was furious. But Hilary hadn't done anything wrong. A marble of sweat rolled down the inside of her purple wool dress, and she tried to look nonchalant. She hadn't done anything wrong. Not a thing. And Stormy was such a stupid dope. She acted like that high school dropout maid was Moses and the Ten Commandments. Everybody knew maids lied. Two boys coughed at the same instant and it sounded like some sort of a signal. The bones in Hilary's back locked. White people never hung black people in trees just for being black. That maid was nuts.

Dana Peabody's tongue drifted upward until it licked the tip of her nose, and her eyes snapped to crossed corners.

Hilary jumped. She hadn't done a thing wrong and Mr. Dunn would protect her. Or would he? Not according to that maid.

And then Dana Peabody whispered "Gotcha!" and spun back around in her seat. She was now holding a small comb between two fingers. She'd just pulled it out of her too tight butt pocket. She wore skintight Jordaches. She'd been struggling to get the comb out. Okay. That meant she wasn't even thinking about Hilary. And the boys in the back of the room were sneaking a game of miniature football. Okay. Their coughing wasn't a signal. It was only to cover up the noise from their game.

"That was very generous of you to volunteer to stay after with the other kids," said Mr. Dunn, squatting next to Hilary's desk. He rested his chin on the back of his hand as he gazed at her. She gave him the smile he wanted. She could go home and watch *Speed Racer*. She wasn't going to be hung.

"We'll make sure you don't miss the late bus," he promised as he moved back toward his desk, but this time it was okay because he wasn't shouting and besides, the noise from rustling notebooks and a boy burping covered him up completely.

1982

COLOR - BLIND

Mabel made a left turn into the grocery store parking lot, flinching behind one of her headaches. She should have sent the new maid, Jackie, on this errand. Except Jackie had the IQ of a rock, and there was no telling what cut of steak she'd have brought back.

Her headache got louder and brighter as she pulled into a space. These people better Watch Out, they were Not going to mess with Mabel Spader today, she Refused to put up with it. She'd do her business and be on her way.

She stood next to her Volvo for a long moment on the pretext of searching for Certs in her handbag. Let them get a good look at her standing beside her luxury car. She sliced the foil wrapper with her nail, dropped a candy in her mouth, and sucked. Two steaks, that was all she needed from these people.

She twisted her ring around so the emerald shone. The

longer she continued to avoid this place, the harder it was to make herself come back. She pulled her coat tighter around her. What was that woman's name? The colored woman who'd refused to give a white man her seat on the bus back in the fifties? Whatever her name was, Mabel could see her footsteps on the pavement as she marched toward the store. We shall overcome. A small voice inside her head reminded Mabel that she Had overcome, or else she wouldn't even be here in the first place, stepping out of a Volvo, and fixing to pay fourteen dollars for two pieces of corn-fed beef.

Electronic doors sprung open as if to rush Mabel toward trouble. A little white boy riding in a cart landed his toy airplane on his mother's handbag and stared at Mabel. Stuck his tongue out. Brat. Her own tongue darted out at the boy of its own accord. Let her get to the meat department. Let her just get to the meat department and get out of this store before she got herself arrested.

Well, hello, how are you, Mabel mouthed at the deaf bakery-department lady as she passed by, lips spreading wide and contracting to tiny *o*'s. Let them see how polite she was to the handicapped. Let them record That in their little ledgers. See this friendly woman in the emerald ring and the cashmere coat, watch this black woman behave better than you do, Mr. Produce Man. She could sense their eyes drilling into the back of her neck as she strolled nonchalantly through their candy aisle toward the back of the store.

Only thing she needed out of this damn place today was the steaks. One aisle away. Two steaks, one for Tina and one for herself. Tina's husband Charlie's latest trick had been to convert to some Arabian religion and put Tina on a diet of steamed vegetables and wheat bread. Each and every time since last October that Mabel and Tina had tried to set up a date for Tina to drive in from Hamden, Tina had mentioned the dribble of fat that had run down her chin after some pork chop she'd snuck, how she'd dreamt about meat for days. Jackie was already preparing the grill, if by some miracle she'd followed the instructions Mabel had tried to drill into her skull before she'd left the house. Tina would have a fit when she saw these steaks Mabel was planning on serving. This store was famous for its Idaho beef. Barry White and steak and baked potatoes, she'd show Tina good living.

She peeked down aisle ten, toward the meat department. Strange voices inside her told her to stop by canned vegetables and get her peas first. To not be a fool, to pull herself together before she embarrassed herself in here again. Mabel wandered toward seafood. Fish might be the better bet. Tina had always liked seafood, and there were plenty of things Mabel could do with some crab legs and butter noodles.

Rosa Parks. That was that woman's name on that bus. Mabel froze in her tracks, clutching her basket. She was lying to herself. Tina couldn't resist fish but she was allergic. Tina would eat the crab legs and break out in hives. The truth was, Mabel was just trying to get by the easy way and avoid that butcher. The fish man knew Mabel. She'd cleared things up with the fish man long ago. One day he'd tried to push his on-sale halibut, and she'd shone her emerald right in his eye.

He'd understood quick that when Mabel Spader said sea bass, she meant sea bass, the same as any white woman. Ever since that day, he'd said nothing but Yes, ma'am as he wrapped her order in paper. But the meat department, that was a whole different story. Mabel took a deep breath as she approached the glass case with its sausages hanging above, Made Fresh Daily For You. Her headache nearly cleaved her in two. Rosa Parks. Rosa Parks.

It was him, the very same butcher who'd been on duty that awful day. She recognized the big red nose, which looked like something ready to cook and serve. He raised an eyebrow to acknowledge her this time. She watched that eyebrow rise and her heart started beating irregularly. It struck her that she might have jumped to conclusions that other, awful day. Probably made a fool out of herself for nothing. No wonder crackers thought all niggers did was complain.

She had the word "steak" halfway hanging in the air before she realized that the butcher's raised eyebrow meant Wait. He reached his clean hands, as she stood there blinking, for a mound of sausage. He molded his fingers through it. He coughed into the crook of his elbow. His hands went back into the sausage. Mabel's body moved when she saw what was happening, but she kept her black mouth shut. Yes, Lord, this was it. The butcher took his sweet time stuffing sausage. Memories flooded her brain.

A crowded evening before a holiday. The butcher tells her she has not been standing there waiting for almost ten minutes. Voice as reasonable as Ronald Reagan claiming welfare mothers drive pink Cadillacs. Tells her to take a ticket and wait her turn behind the other customers. Cocks a fat red ear at the man behind her. Two Cajun marinade pork chops, the man says to the butcher, watching Mabel suspiciously.

Every possible taboo spills out of Mabel's mouth like bile: Black lady. White people. Racist. Five years I've been coming to this Grand Union, she says to a sea of averted eyes, and her tongue won't stop flapping until her voice finally cracks. White folks clear their throats and drift away behind their shopping carts. See no evil, speak no evil. Nausea . . .

A cool, cool rush had washed through Mabel as she'd begun to imagine a stabbing rampage. She'd stabbed every soul in that store, and stabbed her way through the parking lot until she locked herself in her car. Even now, as she stood waiting for the butcher to form his sausages, the thought of murder soothed her migraine somewhat and enabled her to stand there looking pleasant. She whistled at the short ribs in the glass case, but in her mind, she swung a machete. Lord Jesus above in heaven, let some other grocery around here start selling beef this pretty before she ended up in prison.

"Yup." The butcher came to her with bloody hands.

I'd like two good-size filet mignons, Mabel just about let fly out of her mouth. She bit her tongue in a state of near panic. "Filet mignons"—why, some dumb coon who'd never eaten a good cut of meat would say it just that way. "Filet mignon steaks" was on the right track but not quite there. Come on, Mabel, come on, Mabel, the man was waiting, come on. A Pound Of Filet Mignon Cut Into Two Large Pieces? Sliced Into Steaks? A big juicy hamburger after all this time eating nothing but wheat bread and vegetables would probably be just as much a treat for Tina . . . Rosa Parks, Rosa Parks.

"Give me two steaks, that meat right there!"

The butcher smirked as he stuck the meat in the cutter. She fought to keep from breaking into a run out to her car. Sometimes—and maybe this was something she'd get a chance to talk over with Tina, after they'd had their lunch and drunk their glass or two of wine—sometimes she believed that she was losing her mind. Losing. Her. Mind.

It turned out to be one of those days when the sun shot across the sky like a child running out to play. Already two o'clock and Jackie still hadn't gotten the briquettes hot enough to where they could cook a steak. Crème de la Crème Domestics, that was the name of the agency Becka Rainier had suggested Mabel try this latest time. Crème de la Mabel's Behind Domestics. Jackie had the brain of a piece of liver. Becka ought to stick to giving advice about medicine for migraines. Not that Tina was anything but pleased with the hors d'oeuvres and white wine. Tina had died and gone to heaven out here on Mabel's sunporch.

"What did you call this cheese? They need to start selling this at our Shop-Rite in Hamden. So anyway, then Charlie told his supervisor to kiss his ass, and the man said . . ."

Brie off china on a sunporch in Greenwich—it did Mabel's heart good to be able to do this for Tina. She still looked just the same, skinny, too-tight pants under her Muslim habit. Mabel had forgotten how Tina was. Tina got happy, Tina could talk your ear off. Barry White coming through the new speakers made the day feel like a party.

Mabel hadn't let her hair down and relaxed this way in eons. Moody, Hilary'd called her the other day, first in English, then in French. Mabel reminded herself to do some bragging to Tina about how well the kids were doing— Stormy's accelerated math classes up at the university, and Tommytwo turning out to be an athlete. Tina'd be as proud as Mabel. Hilary had some nerve calling Mabel moody, sour-faced as that young lady stayed for no good reason, as popular as she was in school.

Charlie had some CETA job he was hanging on to by the skin of his teeth. You know white folk, she sighed as Tina came around the bend of her story, although it sounded like lazy old Charlie got just what he was asking for. Mabel didn't care if you were Muslim or Chinese, the boss says take inventory, you don't tell him to kiss your ass. Charlie should have taken inventory, gotten his paycheck, and gone and looked for another job. That was exactly what they wanted, that one lazy negro talking about kiss their ass, so they had an excuse to never hire another one. Barry White groaned in the background, and Mabel tapped her foot to the rhythm. Just like old times. Jackie better not forget the chives. Mabel felt like having some chives today.

Jackie banged in through the back door. Mabel peered at the cutting board with the steak on it as Jackie walked toward them on the sunporch. Overdone. Of course. Mabel was coming to the end of her rope with that woman.

"Can you believe he had the nerve?" cried Tina, waving a

hand in the air just as Mabel made the decision to start calling agencies on Monday and get a new girl in here. Mabel had missed something good. That was Tina, waving that hand in the air when things started to get lively.

"What?"

"Charlie reading his supervisor verses out of the Koran!"

"Man must be crazy."

"Excuse me?" Tina lowered her hand and looked at Mabel. Mabel had seen the look before—it was that same look Mabel had to give some of these white women sometimes. Mabel clutched her heart.

She should have been concentrating on this conversation rather than fantasizing about firing Jackie. She hadn't just slipped and called Charlie *lazy,* had she? No, no. She wouldn't have called Charlie lazy, not aloud. Would she? Mabel struggled to remember the exact shape her mouth had taken when she'd spoken a moment earlier. Crazy! Crazy was all she'd said, although she probably should have said brave or even courageous, since Tina was convinced that sloth was a hero. Mabel thanked Jesus she hadn't said lazy. She could fix this, she could fix it.

"You just never know how these white folk will retaliate," Mabel said indignantly. "Charlie was crazy, taking such a big chance."

"Mmm-hmmm." said Tina. She blinked, twice, and the look was erased. Mabel searched Tina's eyes and the corners of her mouth. It seemed to have never been there.

Mabel leaned in closer to Tina, feeling punch-drunk. She watched Tina as she launched into a discussion of how they'd treated Charlie down at the unemployment office yesterday. She watched as intently as if she were putting on lipstick in a mirror, and when Tina told Jackie she better sit her behind down in a chair and have something to eat, Mabel found herself saying Yes. Yes Indeed Jackie, Sit.

This is some good steak, announced Tina, grinning like a child at a birthday party. Mabel smiled back and pointed at a chair for the stunned Jackie to bring over. A migraine rode into Mabel's head like a herd of wild horses as she cut her meat. She waited until the pain got so bad she had to lock herself in the guest bathroom. Dammit, why didn't the woman hurry up and go. Mabel was tired of entertaining. It was all Tina's new religion, it had changed that woman so much they had nothing in common anymore. Mabel shoved bottles aside under the sink, looking for the Fiorinal Becka had told her might make a dent in these headaches.

———

It was a rare magical moment. Brother and sister out on hall passes at the same time, in the same hall. Hilary giggled like crazy when she saw Tommytwo. Trying to walk cool now that he was on the basketball team. She imitated him, even swooped quietly across the hall as if dribbling a basketball. They stuck their tongues out at each other. They wiggled their fingers in their ears.

"Hey!" they whisper-shouted, cracking up at nothing, at the freedom.

Tommy was such a nerdy little brother. No earthly idea how to be cool. It was as simple as that. He was the biggest nerd in the school. He was going to look like such a faggot, out there playing basketball with those bony shoulders. And as A-Team cheerleaders, there was no way that Hilary and Janna Reeves and Martha Duncan could avoid having to cheer for him, even though they were the coolest girls in school.

"Tommy the fruitcake," she always announced when they passed each other in the upstairs hall at home. "Tommy the cherry-blothom bathketball thtar," she lisped at him now. They each smiled big dumpkopf idiot smiles. Hilary tried to turn hers off but couldn't, it was stuck, beyond her control. She grinned like a big goddamn ape at her so-called basketball star of a brother. They threw kicks at each other as they parted. "Tell Mom I've got A-Team practice," Tommy said, showing off, and Hilary flipped him a teeny tiny bird.

Then, a nauseating smell filled the air and that revolting nerd Stormy came bounding around the corner. Woo, wee, good little girly, taking a note to the principal's office.

"Gross." Hilary stepped up to Stormy and poked her in the chest, although it grossed Hilary out to touch her. She smelled dank, in her disgusting black dress that she wore practically every day. She was so damn grotesque it was an embarrassment. Hilary circled her. "Don't you ever brush your teeth?" She had a film on her big buckteeth. Stormy tried to stare her down but eventually chickened out and rolled her eyes and broke away.

"Going to the principal's aww-fisss, good little girl, good little Stormy, good little kiss-ass bitch." Hilary shoved her in the back of her neck with the heel of her hand as Stormy slimed away.

"Fucking bitch," she chopped out the words so they floated in the air after Stormy like soft music. "I think I'll kick your ass today."

"Kiss my tail, you ignorant swine . . . ," and Stormy swished her big pumpkin butt and Hilary wished some big gorilla motherfucker would smack the shit out of her, one of those hard, silent Monkeytown chicks who slept all day in the back of classes and ran track. And all Hilary'd do when she heard about Stormy getting her butt creamed would be to walk up and lob a great gob of lugey on her and say, "Dweeb. You creepy black dweeb. Did I ever tell you I hate you? Oh, by the way, I do hate you." She said it now. And it was a breath of fresh air to speak the truth.

Stormy stopped walking. Like, big deal. Like, let her stop walking, big whoopteedoo. Was that supposed to frighten Hilary? Screw her, if she was mad. Stormy'd called Hilary a hell of a lot worse things than "dweeb," a zillion times. Just her entire attitude. Mommy's good little girl, never got in trouble for anything. If it was Hilary who got straight A's and kissed Mom's butt she could be a math queen too, but who wanted to be a little brownnosing butthole?

"Shove off to the principal's office, so you can kiss his ass too."

But Stormy kept coming. Her tongue bunched up under her lip and she twisted out her neck like a boxer. She pulled back her clawed fist like a bow and arrow . . . she breathed deeply . . . she was going to hit Hilary . . . really hard . . . Daddy said don't act like a bunch of coons! don't act like coons . . .

"I'm your sister!" Hilary wheezed as she slammed into a locker. Stormy's punches were going to break her in two. Stormy's eyes were alive, flashing black marbles as she shoved her fists into Hilary's gut, carving a long hollow pool of pain inside Hilary's stomach. Hilary was gasping on the floor, sprawled on her back.

Stormy clicked away. Hilary heard a football player go "What the fuck?" and she shut her eyes so she couldn't be seen. And in that moment, the hate Hilary had for her sister tripled. She wanted the bitch to get raped by a nigger and left for dead. And somewhere deep inside of her, deep beyond any conscious thought, she added "Don't ever call Stormy 'creepy black dweeb' " to the bottom of a very long list.

———

For Tommytwo, spending the night before his fifteenth birthday over at his good buddy Kazu's house was sort of a mercy thing. Kazu was still a kid. He still spent Friday nights building model planes, for chrissake. Tommytwo was past that stage, way past. As a matter of fact, Kazu as a best friend was turning into a brick around the neck, especially for a guy who'd just made the varsity basketball team as a sophomore. They'd known each other since sixth grade, so it wasn't like Tommytwo would just quit acknowledging his existence. But having a best friend who wore highwater pants and had frosty white zits lined up across his face was starting to become a huge inconvenience. Spending his birthday over at Kazu's was a kind of farewell, Tommytwo's way of saying, You'll always be my bud even though I got cool and you're still an assnose.

"Wanna crank-call Janna Reeves's dad's shop?"

"Is she there tonight?"

"Is she there tonight, is she there tonight," mocked Kazu. "Hell, yeah, she's there."

"Just don't say my name. She knows who I am now, she did a cheer for me at practice."

"Well excuse me, Buttface. Light this clove while I dial. Hello, Mr. Reeves, this is the Internal Revenue Service . . ."

When Tommytwo was a kid, he was a loser just like Kazu, so he had plenty of empathy for the guy. But he'd turned a fateful corner, and nowadays the A-Team coach was flagging him down in the hallway to specially request him to come to tryouts, and Janna Reeves—Janna Reeves!—was writing his name into cheers. Maybe later on he'd tell Kazu how his sisters used to shove him inside the household appliances, and give the poor dope some hope.

"Good night boys," said Kazu's mom. "Happy birthday, Tommy Toe."

The only cool thing about Kazu was his mom, Mrs. Yaki-haro. She was the absolute coolest mom on the face of the earth. She wore her hair long and feathered like girls at school and smelled like Silkience conditioner. Her thick Japanese accent was a definite plus, even though Kazu freaked out every time he heard her say Heh-row instead of Hello. When they were younger, she used to laugh at them spreading peanut butter on their sushi, which she said was the equivalent of dipping it in motor oil. Lately, she'd been reminding him to feel free to call her Mihoko. And he would, too, after he scored his first twenty-point game.

Tommytwo was positive Kazu had never stayed up past ten o'clock, even though he swore he always stayed up forty-eight hours straight during the Jerry Lewis Telethon and saw the naked hula dancer. Per usual, Kazu got his fill of crank-calling every girl in school with a listed number, then tipped back on his pillow and conked out in his retardo cowboy pa-jamas. Tommytwo usually just stripped down to his Fruit-of-the-Looms nowadays, but tonight he wore his old kid-style pajamas too because it was gay to lounge around in under-wear in another guy's bedroom. Good thing he was wearing his pajamas tonight, because Mrs. Yakiharo was peeking through the door now, mouthing, Come see! in between Kazu's off-the-Richter-scale snoring. Tommytwo crept out to the hallway.

"I finished!" she was whispering, in a really happy way, as Tommytwo tiptoed into her studio. He and Kazu used to slide around here in socks. They used to have the best swordfights in the world in this studio, because it was okay to scuff up the walls since they were all covered with paint and plaster of Paris anyway. Mrs. Yakiharo was telling him to shut the door, shut the door, and sweeping her hands together in a particu-larly cute way. She had what might be called a sort of buttony nose. In general, she was a ten, for a mom.

"Now we talk in normal-size voice." She plopped down on a pillow on the floor and set one beside her for Tommy-two. They shot the breeze for a while almost like buddies, and when it came up about Tommytwo making varsity basketball, she clapped her hands and started jabbering in Japanese. It was weird that Kazu hadn't mentioned a big deal like Tommytwo making varsity, since he sure as heck always used to remember to tell Mrs. Yakiharo whenever Tommytwo got jumped for lunch money back in junior high. Overall, Tommytwo was looking forward to not having to deal with that assnose Kazu anymore, not on a regular basis, anyway. He wondered if he should tell Mihoko that her skirt was kind of riding up.

He tried to pay attention to what she was saying and to quit swallowing like a dope fiend. He wondered if girls could tell when a guy checked out their body parts. The more she squiggled around, the more her skirt rode up, and the more he talked about basketball, the more she squiggled around. She sure had interesting legs for a lady that old.

"Coach let me start last game," he told her, swallowing hard when she clapped her hands and wriggled. It was actually a relief when she stood up to unveil her latest piece of artwork and her skirt came tumbling down, since it was weird and sort of incestuous getting choked up about your best friend's mom's knees.

Tommytwo gave her a round of applause when she lifted the sheet off her latest sculpture. Kazu said every guy she sculpted had hair shaped like cauliflower, and it was true, this guy's hair looked like cauliflower too. Kazu thought she must have eaten cauliflower for her first meal in America. As many times as Tommytwo'd been in this studio, he'd never noticed all these busts topped off with cauliflower heads.

What he'd always noticed was that when she sculpted full bodies, she'd sculpt these huge dicks to match. He definitely wasn't gay or anything, but these guys' dicks were too enormous to just overlook. If Tommytwo's mom sculpted guys' dicks, he'd have dropped out of school. Kazu once showed his mom this information pamphlet from health class about teen suicide, and only then did she finally agree to convert a room behind her studio into a storage area for any sculpture with a dick. This new guy had a dick the size of a loaf of French bread. She probably needed help carrying it into the back room, which must have been why she'd summoned him in. Bingo. Her little finger was beckoning.

The room was humonguous for a storage closet. When Mrs. Yakiharo flicked the light, it was like, wow. It wasn't just a closet, it was this whole display room, with burgundy wallpaper and a mirrored wall and spotlights that cut through the dusty air to light each sculpture from below. All these big cauliflower-headed guys' dicks cast sausagey shadows across the ceiling and walls. They were arranged so that each sculpture was a point on a circle and they were facing inward, like Romans watching slaves get torn to pieces by lions. Tommytwo planted Ralph, whom he was holding gingerly by the armpits, in the one empty space.

There was a futon in the middle of the circle. Its sheets were all mussed, sort of the way Mrs. Yakiharo's hair was starting to look as she kind of ran her hands through it and flipped it around. She disappeared behind a panel and suddenly there was noise. Not music exactly, more like jungle drums and screeching monkeys. Tommytwo was a rock-and-roll man himself. He stood there stifling a yawn as he waited to be excused to go back to bed.

She'd forgotten something on the futon. Or something had fallen. One of the dicks had fallen off one of the statues. Tommy strained to count through the dim light. Two, four, six, twelve long purple dicks, twelve cauliflower heads.

"You all right, Tommy Toe," said Mrs. Yakiharo, and the first thing Tommytwo noticed was that she'd spoken her *r* correctly this time, "right," not "light." The second thing he noticed was that the big black dick lying on the futon had a battery pack attached to it. Oh shit, he swore, Oh shit shit shit shit shit. He swerved his eyeballs up to the ceiling and fake-whistled "I Shot the Sheriff." He would have given fifty bucks right then to turn into Spiderman and climb out the window and suction his way down the wall.

What a lousy birthday. Kazu would convulse with a thousand hemorrhages and take the biggest dump in the world if he knew his mom had a frigging battery-operated dildo. The one good thing was that Tommytwo had ridden his bike over so he could just get his stuff and leave. If his own mom had a dildo, jeeze, he couldn't even think about it. He was going to give his mom a hug when he saw her tomorrow morning. She was overall a great mom, he shouldn't kid her so much, teasing her that he was going to tell Dad that Morehouse was eclipsing Princeton as his first-choice college because he wanted to be around their people, stuff like that. If there was a silver lining at all, it was that now he had something to say back when Kazu harped on that time he saw Stormy naked in the bathroom once giving herself a breast exam, if he ever needed to stoop to that level.

She was taking her clothes off. She was taking her clothes off. Kazu's mother was taking her clothes off. Blouse, shoes, skirt—underwear! Uh-oh. Something really weird was going on. He stood there, mouth dropped open.

The door was still ajar. She was closing the door. She was closing the door and now she was locking the door. The door was now locked and Mrs. Yakiharo was completely buck-naked and there was jungle music playing. Tommytwo stood there blinking, terrified.

You too, Tommy Toe, she was saying in this really friendly voice, but it was an order, he could tell. She wanted him to take off his pajamas and lie down on the futon. It was like, she was the mom, so what could he do. He stripped to his underwear. She made a gesture. He thumbed his Fruit-of-the-Looms down to his knees and let them drop. He lay on his stomach, which was the only option, feet toward the dildo in a last ditch effort to pretend he hadn't seen it. Okay, now she was massaging him. Mmm. Okay. Mmm.

Mrs. Yakiharo had hands as soft as Miracle Whip. One side of his brain was going, Get out! Run! She's your best friend's MOTHER. But the other side was hallucinating that he was the sheik in his own palace, somewhere in a lush tropical land with fragrant air. She was Scheherazade, he was Ali Baba, and she'd pulled this bottle of warm oil out of nowhere, like magic. She was rubbing the skin on his ribs between her fingertips and nipping it with her tiny teeth. Her eyes were closed and her lashes were so long they felt like bird wings

ERIKA ELLIS

on his chest. Tommytwo was a goner. Tommytwo was on a whole different, more beautiful planet.

She was licking his chest like ice cream, and here he was all of a sudden, licking her back. Somehow, for the longest second in the world, it mattered more that her skin was deliciously salty than that she was Kazu's mom, or even that Kazu could wake up and start banging on the door at any moment. And the salty skin, man, Tommytwo could have licked it forever.

Except she was biting him harder now, like a dog would, lips snapping shut. She was urging him to bite her back. She actually wanted him to dig his front teeth into her and tear at the skin. It was like, she was the mom, so Tommytwo bit her. This was her house and she wanted to be bitten, so he bit her again and again. The sheik's palace was gone and he'd shrunk back down to being the same Tommytwo his sisters used to stuff into the refrigerator, scared and skittish. If he broke the skin, that would be bad, real bad. She'd take Polaroids of the wounds and tell his parents, Kazu would find out, they'd kick him off the team, maybe kick him out of school altogether, maybe get the police involved. His whole life would be ruined. He concentrated all his energy on toothlessly nipping the skin on her neck. All of a sudden, she reared back and her hair flew up like Catwoman's and she attacked him, slapping him across the face, once, then twice more.

"You hear I say bite me, motherfucker!" shrieked Mrs. Yakiharo, and the next thing Tommytwo knew he was biting her so hard he tasted blood. Spank me was next and then smack my face and then pull my hair and then tie my ankles to some contraption she yanked out from the end of the futon. Tommytwo was horrified and dizzy, but he'd switched to automatic pilot. Fuck me with the dildo and beat me at the same time then eat me then beat me then eat me then beat me . . .

Tommytwo did it all, did it twice, his body working in ways it had never worked before, one ear cocked for Kazu. Mrs. Yakiharo clicked a pair of black steel handcuffs out of thin air. Tommytwo cuffed her wrists and roped her ankles, silently, quickly. Despite his fear, when the time came he fucked her, because what the heck else was a guy supposed to do.

The phone was ringing when Tommy rolled his bike into the garage early the next morning. He fumbled with his keys and stumbled inside to catch the next ring because a frantic little birdy was telling him he'd better not let Mom or Dad answer it. It sounded like a crank at first, some little kid sucking a balloon. Sounded like a guy's face being pulled through rubber. The only reason he didn't hang up was a single note he recognized, a fragment of a voice as familiar as the voice of anyone in his family. He froze. He grabbed his chest and just stood there, listening to Kazu gasping for breath on the other end of the line.

"Hey, man, is it true, man? Answer me, is it true, man? Answer me goddammit!"

"What the heck are you talking about," Tommytwo choked out. "Man, you're a lunatic calling here this early."

"Tommytwo, is it true, man? Am I going nuts? Did that happen? Did you fuck my mom, man?"

"You're nuts, man!" said Tommytwo, even managing a sickly little laugh on top.

"Did you and my mom have sex?" Kazu screeched like stained glass shattering. Mrs. Yakiharo was crying in the background, and the dog was barking and it sounded like purgatory and Kazu slammed the phone down hard. Tommytwo fell against the barstool, batting at his head with a hard fist. Which is when his dad walked in whistling "I'm on Top of the World!" by the Carpenters or Abba or one of those sixties groups.

"There's that damn cat again, pissing in the tulips." Dad was gazing out the window as he worked a shred of sausage from between his teeth with a matchstick, and he had Lecture Time written all over himself. Fuck.

"Happy birthday, son," said Dad, wrapping his legs around a stool and patting the one next to him. Tommytwo concentrated on taking slow breaths, one after the other. This could not be happening. Tommytwo very casually got himself a plate of hash from the skillet on the burner and pulled his stool up close to the phone, willing it not to ring again, not yet.

"Thanks, Dad." Memories of last night were whipping through his brain like hurled jackknives. Mihoko's nipples were redder and sharper than middle fingers. She had growled deep in her throat and kept lunging at him, all night long, like machinery come alive in a horror movie. The girls better not be hogging the bathrooms all day; he was desperate to wash. Oh God. Kazu knew.

"You're not a boy anymore," Tommytwo's dad said out of

the blue and Tommytwo nearly fell off his seat thinking he was about to get deep-fried. He calmed down when he realized his father was still absorbed with the Kennedys' cat out the window, revving himself up to dish out a healthy serving of unsolicited advice.

Tommytwo'd screwed up majorly. He felt like smothering himself in the oven. He eyed the broiler knobs as his dad started upchucking his usual birthday lecture a chunk at a time. It was the same old one about how he'd already saved up half his college tuition by his sixth birthday by working ninety-nine hours a day after school, which he had to walk four hundred miles to, barefoot and backwards. How he'd planned all his fabulous success way back in the womb when he was the wonder fetus.

Yeah, yeah, first black butcher at the stockyard, only negro enrolled, first negro at the law firm, ten hard years in the basement office, blah blah blah, yadduh, yadduh, yadduh. Twenty-five birthday bucks today, Tommytwo predicted. All this reminiscing about his broke era meant Dad was not coming off of any cash, and that was all it meant to Tommytwo.

Hilary had this loofah sponge upstairs which she used to keep hanging in the shower until the time she caught Stormy using it and freaked. Tommytwo knew where she kept it, and he was going to get it and scrub himself hard, especially his dick. He was going to scrub this fucking dick right off. Oh God, what had he done? He deserved to be shot, he deserved to be SHOT.

Now his dad had a whole second plate of fried potatoes and was launching into the Learn-from-the-knowledge-I've-accumulated subsection of the speech, which Tommytwo knew so well he could have set it to music. Don't blame others for your problems, kum-ba-ya, old porch monkeys wasting their lives rocking in their chairs ought to get off their tired asses, kum-ba-ya, don't come grabbing on my coattails, oh, oh, kum-ba-ya. This speech in particular always pissed Tommytwo off. Dad was from the Stone Age, the knowledge he'd accumulated was about as useful today as an eight-track tape. He felt like telling his dad he'd spent his entire birthday night getting more or less assaulted by his best friend's mother. See what Dad thought about that.

"I've got bite marks on my ass," he wished he had the guts to say to his dad, who could have been alone in the room chatting with his mirror. He was sick and tired of his dad's stupid fucking monologues. Tommytwo watched his dad's mouth bow in and out, wide, then small, like one of those finger toys the girls used to make in elementary school. They'd hold it out for a guy to lift the flap and read the message, which was inevitably You Suck!

"I made myself a plan, not like some of these coons out there"—Dad plunged his pinky into the kitchen counter and fingered up some invisible morsel—"digging the gristle out of their pork chops," droned Dad, and it suddenly occurred to Tommytwo that he wasn't a virgin anymore. He'd been shuttled from boyhood into manhood without even realizing it. A guy waited all his life for this day. Devoured by somebody's really cute mom on his fifteenth birthday? And he was upset about it? What was wrong with him, for chrissake. Any red-blooded American guy knew losing it was way more important than where or how, as long as there were no house pets involved, no raped pooches. She was a beautiful older woman. Guys prayed for that kind of luck, and here he was upset. He wondered, frantically, if he was gay. He shuffled the guys on the team through his head, wondering how many suspected.

"See these hands?" His father suddenly shoved his hands at Tommytwo and flexed them right under his nose, so close Tommytwo could smell the sausage. Oh God, this was the absolute worst part, the magic-splinters routine. It seemed like Tommytwo had had a hundred million private viewings of the stupid black pinpoints that became visible beneath the skin if Dad had his flashlight handy, which he always did. Remnants from way back during his soul-edifying cotton-picking days as a wonder fetus in the fields of Mississippi before he'd met Mom. He watched his dad pick at his palm with his thumbnail. "No silver platters like you kids. And if I don't make it all the way through, son, you'll be handed down the mantle," said Dad. Frantic to stop Dad before he launched into the Your Responsibility As Heir To My Dream addendum, Tommytwo broke in:

"Wow, Dad, you've lived a truly remarkable life." He poked at the splinters, grimacing and even throwing in a couple of small groans. It worked like music on a savage beast. Dad was packing up his show, squeezing Tommytwo's shoulders, setting his plate in the sink, and twisting his tie up to his throat.

"Vision, son. Courage. Perseverance. And I'll tell you something else, Tommy boy. Imagination. Ingenuity."

"I'll have to write that down, Dad," said Tommy, easing off the stool as if he were more concerned with stretching his legs than with getting the hell out of Dodge. As for Kazu, he'd deny everything, for Kazu's own peace of mind. It would be his final parting gift to his childhood friend: a tiny seed of doubt planted, that perhaps Tommytwo had not boned Mihoko. Oh man, if Tommytwo's mom was that kind of slut . . . Tommytwo couldn't even bear to think about it. Yes, he'd deny everything and keep Kazu from having to live a completely worthless life. Then he'd ride his bike around to a couple of the guys on the team's houses and let word seep out that he'd had an extremely memorable night with a mysterious older woman who'd wanted him bad, real bad.

"My little good girl, my sweet little Stormy. Girl, give Mama a hug. I'm so proud I could burst wide open. I never knew my baby had it in her. Oh, I knew you were smart, but you caught colds so often as a small girl, I was sure you'd missed something . . ."

"Math genius, that's my girl. Now go on, here comes your bus to UConn. Give Pops a hug."

"We love you, my angel!"

"Bye, Mom, bye, Dad!"

Stormy found a seat on the bus and watched her parents waving on the lawn. How did she ever get strapped with a family like this. Mabel Aggie did the thing where she scratched the back of her head in a certain way that looked to Stormy like a baboon scratching his big red ass. At which point Uncle Tom dragged her inside before the neighborhood's early risers saw his wife pulling out chunks of hair, blissed out on painkillers at seven A.M. He should have left her at the side of the road shelling peas when they met. Stormy sure as heck got the pick of the litter when it came to parents. Two prize pups. A few more months before she turned eighteen and could flee this hellhole for New York City.

She could strangle herself for having skipped school the day they explained the ups and downs of acing the math placement test. If she'd known it meant something, she would never have let herself get caught in this predicament. Superlative math skills, superlative math skills. She would rather have had two size thirty-four double-Ds and a mane of Tommytwo's curly hair. Big thrill, she got to get up at the crack of dawn twice a week and chitchat with the Munsters and catch a bus to—whoopteedoo—our famous, barely accredited UConn, thank you very much. And take a math class with a worm-brained nerd who thought he was a psychic genius.

Hilary and the rest of the retards got to stay back at high school and take algebra with Mr. Kinkaid. French Mr. Kinkaid from Paris, the kind of teacher a girl could practice her flirting techniques with and see instantaneous results. Girls in Mr. Kincaid's class—the ones with nerve—weren't wasting their lives away, the way Stormy was in honors math, and that was a stone-cold fact.

Nobody knew, but this was how bizarre Stormy was: She

had these long-drawn-out conversations with her various body parts. She was at this very moment conversing with her hair as the bus lurched around curves. She was telling it, Don't frizz up. She hated it for revolting against her on misty mornings, getting hard and cubic around the edges, like helmets the guards at Buckingham Palace wore. You better not do it today, she warned. She hated her hair, hated its guts.

There were three body parts that she was not on speaking terms with absolutely at all: both cheeks of her butt and her left boob. It was the only butt she'd ever seen that stuck out of a back like a pumpkin propped on a shelf. And her left boob. Stupid piece of malformed fat. Practically concave, goddammit. No wonder those jerk-offs in trig acted like she had leprosy. Between her hair and her vital statistics, she was barely even female.

Her posture sucked lemons. She snapped at her spine, told it to sit up straight, but it was stubborn. It stayed slumped until she happened—thank God—to notice Roscoe glancing her way in the rearview mirror. Always be kind, that was her golden rule when it came to men, even jerk-offs. Even if she didn't want Roscoe, he was the first pony in what was eventually going to grow to a stable of male admirers. Over half of Marilyn's biographers were her unrequited admirers.

Those two cornballs she hung around with on days she went to school knew there was a guy who had a crush on Stormy, somebody she saw Tuesdays and Thursdays when she went to UConn. But she hadn't said he was the bus driver and she definitely hadn't said his name was Roscoe. Screw them. She could hear Emily now, humming the Wedding

March, bugging her to go hang out at the bridal shop at the mall. She was sick of those dopes, always massaging their egos with their pathetic "We may not be having sex yet, but you can bet we'll be the first to find husbands." If they kept nagging her to tell who the guy was, she'd make up a name, Artie or something else unmistakably lily-white, and see if they thought to hum anything then. Who wanted to get married, anyway? Not Stormy, and certainly not to one of these average Neds around here who couldn't even dream bigger than a stint at Yale and a three-car garage.

Out of everyone on earth, the person she hated most was that nurse who'd pressed her hands down all the girls' backs for scoliosis yesterday and warned them that two out of ten of them would end up like that frigging crooked old hag in that commercial if they didn't drink their goddamn milk. Stormy hated people like that nurse, always ready to whisper some horrible news in your ear, reminding you that you better move faster because your time was ceaselessly, continuously running out. Every girl in PE, even Her Beauteousness, Hilary's favorite ass-kiss recipient, Janna Reeves, had hung around in the girls' room afterward and stressed out about the possibility of ending up zipped into a tin can for five years.

And even after the doctors finally popped you out with their giant can opener after your spine unraveled, a crippled aura would hang on you the same way a smelly yellow aura still hung on Kaitlyn Hunter, who once peed on herself in a big way in the seventh. Just like boys kept lists of the girls who gave blow jobs, girls were always whipping out photo albums full of dog shots of other girls. There were tons of backstabbing wenches who kept cameras in their lockers, lying in wait for their so-called best friends to show up at school with dandruff standing out like sugar on their black sweaters. Which was exactly why Stormy didn't let them take her school picture for the yearbooks and why she didn't put a whole lot of stock in best friends. When she wasn't hanging out with those dopey sugar-sweet bridesmaids, she was a loner, because she had dreams so big these Greenwich jerk-offs would get vertigo just imagining.

Scoliosis. Man oh man, just what Stormy needed. And if it was communicable at all, no doubt it was by now fungusing and flowering all up her back. She could still feel those powdery palms tapping her, searching for disease. School sucked! People were always tapping at you, always shoving you into whichever corner they thought you belonged in. Probably the biggest thing that was casting a shadow over her whole life was yet something else that had happened, where else, at school: that stupid garbage that Mr. Worm Brain said the second week of trig class at UConn. It still haunted her, she still bolted awake from nightmares. Maybe it gave him a kick to ruin kids' lives, made him feel like a man or something. His big dopey grin, his stupid predictions for their future, she hated him. Brad Hollister, according to Worm Brain, was going to be head of the World Bank someday. Big whoop, what loser would want to spend his life wearing three-piece suits and worrying about money. Stormy's fate was even duller. Who the hell wanted to be the best math teacher in Connecticut. Not Stormy Spader. Screw Connecticut. She had way much more up her sleeve than being a math teacher in

Connecticut. She wiggled her spine up straight, bouncing high into the air as the bus hit a speed bump.

As long as she lived, she'd never forget the time she saw Suzanne Pleshette at the grocery store. It was absolutely an unforgettable moment, a turning point in Stormy's life. The aisles were clogged with voyeurs watching her push her cart through the fruit-and-vegetable department, not an eyeball in the place glued on anything but her. The butcher came out swiping his hands on his bloody apron like he'd won the Academy Award when Ms. Pleshette set a steak in her cart. Screw being anybody's stupid math teacher. She'd rather give herself a whiskey enema than be a math teacher. She'd be flinging kisses out of a silver screen someday, that's where she'd be, if any of these numbskulls ever bothered to ask.

Roscoe the bus driver winked at her in his rearview mirror. Even on days when her hair was staging one of its coups d'état, there was Roscoe, one eye winking. He was the only black guy she really knew, except her brother, and the only guy in Greenwich who recognized that Stormy had a certain air about her that left supposed beauty queens like Janna Reeves—blah!—in the dust. Roscoe was actually sort of a fox, if she left him in her peripheral vision. His muscles were as big as frigging grapefruits. His biggest problem, besides the fact that he spoke excruciating English, was that he always left his mouth hanging open and it made him look slightly mentally retarded. She'd always been sort of repulsed by him, until today.

She could see his rosy tongue weaving over his thick juicy lips in the rearview mirror as he tilted his head to watch passengers exiting from the rear. She wondered if he'd be good in bed. Black guys were supposed to be wild animals. Janna Reeves's sister slept with one once and told Janna his dick was over fourteen inches long, which Stormy oohed and aahed over like everyone else in the girls' room that day, even though a two-inch tampon was actually bad enough. Stormy had no idea how long Roscoe's dick was since she'd never had a bigger conversation with him than Transfer? No, thanks. If she was ever going to see it, something was going to have to happen soon, because there was no way she was taking this trig class for a whole year, even if she was supposed to get a plaque at graduation. Screw a plaque. She was going one semester, to get Aggie and Uncle Tom off her case. Beauty sleep was infinitely more important in the long run, no contest.

There had to be other girls in her boat, Scarlett O'Hara souls trapped in Prissy bodies, who practically had to have money hanging out of their pockets for a guy to look at them. Then again, the one and only cool old lady in the world, Helen Gurley Brown, said every girl had unlimited potential. She said just hang around football games and learn a first back from a first down and you'd be fighting guys off. According to *Cosmopolitan* magazine, an apple a day keeps the doctor away and a risk a week keeps a girl at her sexual peak. *Cosmo* was her bible, but to this day, Stormy had never watched one football game or taken one single solitary risk.

She was going to do it. She dropped her chin so nobody could see and practiced sensuously gliding her tongue over her lips. She chewed away the bits of chapped skin and tried it again. She was going to lick her lips at Roscoe. She was actually going to do it. Drop the hyperventilation bit, she ordered her lungs.

By the time Roscoe cranked the bus to a stop at UConn with his powerful blue-collar arms, Stormy was ready. She waited—a girl should never let a potential guy see her rushed or frazzled—as the UConn dopes bopped out; then she picked up her book bag. Roscoe was watching her in his rearview mirror, she could see his bushy black brows holding steady. This was her stop and he knew it. All this electricity was zooming down the aisle from him to her, bam! bam! bam! Her hair stood on end from the static, which it could only do if it was bone-dry and bone-straight, and she thanked it effusively for not napping up, promised it an avocado treatment.

Whoops. She'd let the sand run out of the hourglass, she'd waited that one moment too long. All the real people left on the bus after the students got off were craning their necks around to see what dopey kid was holding things up, making them late for their little jobs and appointments. Talk about embarrassment, every eye on the bus was watching her. She hoisted her bag onto her shoulder and took a couple of steps, planning on ducking out the back.

They were still watching. Everybody. This one guy in a handicapped seat with a whiplash collar stood up just to shift his butt sideways and watch her. Maybe she was . . . maybe for once she looked . . . even Heather Constantine had told her she had humongous eyes, that time in the locker room when everyone was putting on makeup before the Rockfest. Cow eyes, Heather had said, which sounded like an insult but was actually not. Screw it. She was going to walk that walk, all the way up to the front, and when she got to the turnstyle she was going to lick her lips and say Thanks for the ride, Roscoe, in a double-entendre sort of way that would knock him flat.

Stormy held her chin high and begged her pumpkin butt to do a Marilyn Monroe. Just like clockwork, it swished inside her chinos, tick tock, tick tock, as she meandered up the aisle. The whole bus was frigging captivated by her, it was a stunning moment, history being made. Suzanne Pleshette was a Kansas City hick compared with Stormy. It hit her that an oversized butt did not necessarily have to be a handicap and neither did lopsided boobs, not if a girl knew how to *move.*

One after another, she began to drop specially selected smiles down onto each rider. One for the salesman with the curly snail of a mustache, who had the aura of a guy who slept with blow-up dolls. He blinked about forty times in one second. Another for two scummy brothers in matching checked jackets and ties. Each rider perked up as she passed, she was a priest lighting candles. Her butt was keeping time, her eyes were huge, her hair was Lustrasilk. She was beautiful. She was wonderful. She was perfection. She quickly counted the days since her last touch-up—only thirteen!— and right there in the aisle, she struck a pose, dropped her neck and flipped her head, feeling triumphant as the hair whispered back into place. A kid up front whistled, and his grandma smacked him.

Shit. There were the two blond guys with the corny buzz haircuts from her trig class in the senior-citizen seats near the front, poking at one another behind creepy Cheshire cat grins. She must be going blind not to have seen them. One was Mr. Glow Worm's pet, the next Neil Armstrong, and his friend was the one with the telltale uphill handwriting of a nuclear physicist. Hello, total and complete embarrassment. They were right there, feet sticking a kilometer out into the aisle, knees bouncing under books she recognized from class. No way she could avoid them. All she knew was that if Helen Gurley Brown were here, she'd say Go for the libido.

Neil Armstrong's eyes were glued to the switch of her hips, which was transforming into something spastic. Nigger nigger nigger nigger, the nuclear physicist whispered at her, softer than the lion's purr of the bus engine, but she heard it like a gunshot, felt it like she'd been shoved over the edge of a cliff. Happened just that quick—wham bam thank you ma'am—and it was over and nobody else could possibly have heard anything more than a hum. But there were his corn-yellow teeth, gleaming at her gleefully now, and his eyes, roaming her face, searching for a reaction, as if he'd asked her a riddle. Keep smiling, she ordered her cheeks, which were so fucking lame they were quivering. You stay up there, she demanded of the tears that had heated instantaneously to the sizzling point like drops of oil in a scalded pan. I hate you, she yelled in her mind, and it echoed all through her body.

"See you again Thursday, sweetheart," said Roscoe, licking his chops.

Stormy pinched a "Bye" out between her frozen lips, wishing wishing wishing she'd never ever left her room today.

———

The phone rang at nine A.M. That's how they did. People around here had no respect for a Sunday morning. Had to be Becka Rainier, calling to tell about her weekend in New York with her Mexican *amore,* wanting Mabel's dose of absolution.

Mabel watched the telephone ring itself stupid. Rang until the whole room lay shaking. This was Mabel's time, these people didn't pay her enough to work for them on Sundays. And it was work sometimes, listening to these white women complain. And lie—Lord but white women could lie. Becka had found the only Mexican in Connecticut to have an affair with, but still she clung to her same lie about not seeing color, as if it were scripture from the Bible. Mabel did not have the energy to toe anybody's color-blind line today. No, not on a Sunday morning.

Where was Mabel's Fiorinal, it wasn't in the bedside table drawer. Dimes to dollars, the new maid, Eliza, had found it and stolen it. Woman was slinking around here lately like some kind of animal, face just as long. Thought nobody suspected her of stealing. Thought somebody would feel guilty for suspecting her because she was black. She'd better think again.

The phone rang eight times before Mabel started wondering how in the world Becka had pulled off a weekend in New

York with Felipe, anyway. Becka, entrenched in the throes of early menopause, was dressing that same sleazy way Cher had started dressing after Sonny ran out on her, and was back smoking. Old Chas Rahnyay had enough brains to figure out that his wife's spur-of-the-moment weekend in New York in tight leather pants meant more than a shopping spree, they didn't make a man a judge for having pretty blue eyes. Old Chas pretended he heard no evil, saw no evil, but that man knew exactly what was going on, white men were like that. Mabel picked the phone up on ring ten, already smelling the scent of Becka's new musk perfume.

"Yoo-hoo," Becka said.

"How was your weekend?"

"It was GLORious, where should I start?"

Becka revved up her monologue with what sorts of crotchless underclothes she had bought for her weekend with Felipe, and Mabel's mind drifted back to the only time she'd insisted on taking the babies home to Lovejoy. Daddy had just bought that new television set and he'd watch it all day long. Called himself monitoring whitey.

Daddy got ugly whenever Walter Cronkite came on. Daddy hated Walter Cronkite. Ig'nant even for a white man, he'd say to Mabel's babies, who thank God were too young to understand his drivel. Daddy'd talk right over Walter Cronkite, give his own editorial. As far as Daddy was concerned, everything from the Angela Davis trial to Nixon sending more troops to Vietnam was linked back to the white man who'd run over Daddy's foot when he was yay high.

Man wouldn't slow his car down, no siree. Plymouth the

same manila color as the uniforms they'd worn in Germany, and couldn't stop and give a colored boy a ride to the hospital. Just rolled down the window and threw out a sock. White folks some evil cusses, Daddy would punctuate the story, snapping his fingers at the babies to make sure they stayed awake. Just threw Daddy a sock out the window and told him to hobble on home and have his mammy fix him up. A sock, Daddy would tell those babies, again and again until they shouted it back to him. Daddy teaching her babies to see his brick walls, even more so than the high cost of plane fare with three children, was exactly why Mabel had never insisted on taking the babies back to Lovejoy again.

"So I tell Felipe my fantasy, remember? the one where I kind of sashay into a smoky nightclub, and I run my fingers through my hair and he grabs me and starts licking my armpits like a man possessed? So I'm telling Felipe the fantasy, and we're in a bar, and I happen to be wearing my red dress, my sleeveless . . ."

Mabel shuddered to think of someone licking that woman's old pruny armpit, held the phone far enough from her ear that she could just barely hear. Becka must realize that while she was handing Mabel all of her business on a silver platter, Mabel never gave a thing back. Which wasn't right. It was nothing but that same old negro pessimism Daddy and the rest of them had tried to instill in Mabel as a child. Here she was living proof that Martin Luther King's dream had come true. Negro and caucasian living in the same community, walking hand in hand to the mountaintop. And at the same time, she was holding the phone pinched between two fingers, nothing but cynical as she pictured some poor Mexican's tongue in that white woman's underarm.

She ought to try sharing some personal business with Becka. That might quench this feeling that somebody amongst them was getting used. She could offer up what had happened the other night at the annual ABA banquet, when her pantyhose split up the side. Every color of woman in the rainbow had thigh issues. No need to tell her all the *white* people had heard the rip and turned to stare, she'd just say *people;* the main point was still there, if not the bite.

Of course, what she felt like telling Becka was what happened just the other day. What made white folk so hateful? That Vietnamese girl who did Mabel's pedicures, she'd talk in Vietnamese about how bad a woman's feet were right in front of her face. But white folk—please. White folk took the cake. New girl working at the post office and Mabel'd made the mistake of walking out of the house without her birthday ruby. What Mabel felt like doing was having a good long conversation with Becka Rahn-yay about what white folk would put a woman through, about how come Mabel still had to wear jewels to the post office to get treated with common decency after six years. Talk about rocking the boat. That boat would capsize if some of the things that ran through Mabel's mind started leaking out.

"Listen, Mabel, I shouldn't even be mentioning this."

Girl, you might as well go ahead . . .

"Okay, can you still hear me? I'm standing in the closet."

"Becka? Can't you talk a little louder? Is Chas in the room?"

"Mabel, can you hear me? Listen, Tom's going to be made a partner!"

"What?"

"A partner at his firm! They finalized the decision last night!"

"Excuse me?"

"Thomas Spader, his name will be right on the letterhead!"

"My Tom's going to be a partner?"

"Yeesssss!"

"Aaaah!"

Half that aaaah was real. Half was politics plain and simple, but half was real. Every step that man had taken, he'd practically had to use karate. He worked a hundred hours a week for those people, partnership was the least he deserved. And not one thank-you from black folk the whole journey, either, not one photograph in *Ebony* or even *Jet*. Somebody had been watching over Tom Spader to let him swim this far against the tide. Mabel just hoped it was Jesus, and not the other fellow with the horns. Quit being blasphemous, she snapped at herself. Becka was still on the line, back adding something in about Felipe.

Mabel's head was clear and her mind was moving at its regular pace through mundane topics. Remember to unplug some of those cords from the extension thingamajig before they got set afire in their sleep. Tell Eliza to pick up a bag of potatoes at the supermarket. Be a miracle if that girl would deign to wrap them in some tinfoil and stick them in the oven without expecting overtime pay. Woman's attitude was no doubt connected to that two-bit Jamaican diploma hanging downstairs on a nail nobody had given her permission to bang into the wall. And that Becka had talked about everything from anal sex to the price of tea in China before she happened to mention Tom made partner.

Car needed washing. Find the pumice stone. Eliza hid it in a different location every day just to vex her and Mabel never said a word. No reason to give her the pleasure of thinking Mabel had feet so full of corns she needed to know where her pumice stone was twenty-four hours a day, seven days a week. And that Becka had stood in her closet to tell the news, as if Mabel's own husband making partner was even less Mabel's business than some Mexican man licking Becka's armpit. Tom Spader would be a ball of wire tonight when he came home, make them all nervous wrecks. And who had told her little white self anyway? Chas Rainier wasn't even associated with Tom's firm, unless there was some underground connection. Which there undoubtedly was.

"I'm speechless. I'm just, I'm so excited I can hardly think!" Mabel said through clenched teeth. No need to have this woman thinking niggers were too stupid to know how to react to good news.

"It's wonderful! I know exactly how you feel. Chas says we're going to throw him a party ..." Colored women dressed like babydolls in lace aprons specially hired to carry in platters of cucumber sandwiches, Becka's boy's graduation picture in the mahogany frame with the eyes that followed you around the room, no music going, never any music. Too much butter in the sandwich, the men licking it off their hands, and that damn cocker spaniel slipping in when the door opened and flinging himself on folks' pantyhose and shredding them to ruin.

"Oooh, a party."

They'd already had their little party to make Tom partner, she would bet her bottom dollar. Mabel thought about their circle of associates sometimes and pictured a whole coven of witches, rubbing their big chalky hands, Chas Rahnyay done up in a white beard long as Moses'. She got her datebook and penciled in "Rainier" two Saturday nights away, then begged off the phone with some mess about having an appointment to go get a wash and set. As if anybody in this godforsaken town would know the first thing about giving Mabel a wash and set her fifth week into a touch-up.

"Children!"

The girls' heads poked out of their rooms, and Tommy-two's from around the third-floor bannister. Towel around Stormy's neck was green from two-dollar-apiece avocado, which Mabel had told her time and time again not to go wasting on her hair.

"Girl, what did I tell you about the avocado?"

"I bought it with all my own money! Maaaaammm! I neeeed that!"

"All you kids come here and listen to me. I said come over here and listen. I have some good news to tell you about your daddy."

"Ouch!"

"Stand up straight, young lady, do you want curvature of the spine? And you, Miss Attitude, may you be so kind as to tell me what this is I'm looking at?"

"Mon gilet du cheerleading," Hilary muttered in that French couldn't nobody understand.

"Excuse me?"

"I said, it's my cheerleading sweater, Mother."

"Wrong, it's my sweater, your father and I paid that ridiculous amount of money for it and you have the nerve to be wearing it over a nightgown? Do you hear me talking to you?"

"I was cold."

"And what's this on the sleeve? Is this jelly? Is this jelly on this sweater?"

"Ow!"

"And you, young man, I don't ever want to find one more Morehouse catalogue lying around this house. Are you trying to give your poor father a heart attack? That man has slaved all his life so his son could go to a Princeton or a Yale. And here you children are, throwing it in his face."

"It was only a practical joke—"

"You children are one slim generation from nothing, one sli-i-imm generation from no college education, from no Pinto, from no such thing as any ski trip to Vermont, a generation from nothing but misery, do you hear me talking? And here you are, three of the few black children living the American dream."

"Toujours colour," muttered Hilary.

"Excuse me?"

"Nothing."

"That's it. Go get the belt."

"Huh?"

"I said go get the belt. GO GET ME A BELT! Are you deaf?"

"A belt? What for?" Stormy whispered to her brother.

They'd see what for. They'd see exactly what for. Walking around here with these long faces when they ought to be ecstatic, that was what for. Phone rang fifteen times this morning, fifteen times, and not one of them could crawl out of bed to answer it now that they had their own phone line. Pinto in high school, and all these girls could say was where were the leather interiors, that was what for. These children ought to be down on their knees giving thanks. Mabel palmed the buckle and wound leather around her fist.

They hovered against the wall. Mabel whipped and whipped. She should have whipped them long ago. Four hundred dollars' worth of cheerleading uniforms for Miss Smartmouth, and now she's got the letter sweater on over her nightgown—Because She's Cold!—and elbow just full of jelly. Mabel planted her feet apart and swatted harder and each stroke was like a spoonful of honey being poured into her very soul. Mabel flung the belt down the stairway and stomped back to her room, feeling at peace for the first time in a long time without the aid of prescription drugs.

"What the heck was that all about?"

"PMS?"

"My God, how weird."

1985

WALLS COME
TUMBLING DOWN

Satin sheets, yes indeed. Mabel felt as if somebody had been keeping secrets from her all her life. She slid her feet and her ankles and her shins all the way to up her thighs in as if she were coated in oil. Yes, ma'am, Sateen brand. That company ought to call Mabel and have her star in their commercial.

Mabel had bought that lying *Redbook* for the last time. That story about empty-nest syndrome must have been put in to scare readers. Supposedly a woman jumped out of her bathroom window when her boy left for Brown University. Mabel had cut that article out and braced herself. The morning that Hilary drove back to Wellesley, Mabel'd got herself a kettle of hot tea and set her bottle of Fiorinal beside her and even set her blood-pressure kit on the counter.

The article said to confront the grief head-on, so Mabel had sat there in the kitchen and forced herself to reminisce: Hilary was a senior this year at Wellesley. Mabel remembered when

Miss Smartypants was five years old, first learning to read. And Stormy had her own apartment near UConn now and was talking about continuing her education studying art in Europe. Little Tommytwo, her baby, was finally off to More-house. And to tell the truth, Mabel was proud to think of him at Morehouse, although it was still proving to be a very hard pill for his father to swallow.

It wasn't often that Mabel went looking for depression, but she'd done it that day. Must have been a white woman afflic-tion, that empty-nest syndrome, because Mabel felt nothing but the peace and contentment of a job well done. She'd seen a rainbow that day, it was that kind of day. More than crying, Mabel had felt like driving out to the mall. They'd had a satin sale on at Macy's, just one queen-sized left and all the rest twin. Seemed like fate.

Mabel stretched, swimming in the cool fabric. She let her new Puerto Rican woman, Joyce—Mabel couldn't pronounce whatever it was the woman called herself in Spanish—wash them and put them right back on each week. It turned out satin sheets made a woman lazy. Made a woman want to spend every day shopping for silky things to wear to bed so that she could rub her body against the slipperiness. Made a woman feel like a woman.

And satin caused certain changes in a man too. Twenty-five years, and he'd never interrupted her *Johnny Carson* to make love like he was doing tonight. All this sighing and coughing as if he suddenly couldn't sleep with the television on, after twenty-five years. She yawned and flicked the remote and smiled into her pillow. And here came his toe, nudging at her ankle. Mabel kept smiling into the pillow.

"Have you ever seen a judge's mallet?"

"No, sir," said Mabel. She just couldn't bring herself to say Your Honor, the way she knew he wanted. She couldn't understand why it excited him so to be on the shortlist for McCollush's seat on the bench. Those people were never going to let him have that seat, not for long. Just like that Judge Hastings down in Florida, they'd find a way to bring him down once they got tired of him trying to change the system to help black folk. And he'd better get a signed guarantee that the firm would keep sending his stockholder dividends. Long-standing customs could end on a whim where negroes were involved.

"Ever been devoured by a judge, young lady?"

It seemed like now, what with all the commotion and the luncheons and he'd even had that radio interview on WYBC where they'd jumped the gun and called him the first black judge in the district, she would have assumed that a man who normally . . . did it . . . once every two or three weeks would be doing it even less. Yet here it was midnight after yet another five-hundred-dollar plate of chicken Kiev and here was Mabel, flat on her back, legs doing the splits. Tom's head was a nubbly globe beneath her satin nightgown, where he was down doing his business.

She kept both eyes glued on the gold glint of doorknob in the dark, willing the FBI not to come bursting in. The sun rose and set on oral loving, according to Becka Rainier. And another fan was the loudmouthed girl who'd been Mabel's last try at a live-in. My man got to know how to eat him some peaches, Mabel had heard that girl tell somebody over the phone one day in her hard voice. My nigger need to know how to use that tongue and get himself all down in some peaches, yassum. Had the nerve to smack her lips, right there in front of Mabel's children. That was one girl who hadn't lasted long, not in Mabel's house. Mabel mostly felt sorry for Tom down there.

A woman couldn't help but wonder what she looked like from that angle. Mabel squeezed her eyes tight, trying to squash out pictures of fat, purple salt-water octopuses sliming their tentacles around wet Bermuda onions as Tom made his noises. It was plain that the only way she was going to get through this tonight was the same way she always did, concentrating on things outside this bedroom. As she found herself doing so many times a day, Mabel turned her mind to her new neighbors, the Crisps in the colonial on the corner, the powder blue.

The Crisps and their flower cuttings sitting in jars on a metal table they'd dragged into the yard. Mrs. Kennedy must be rolling in her grave to see those countrified negroes all over her property. The old Crisp man, the grandfather, actually sat outside and rocked in his lawn chair all day every day. Mabel'd seen him go into what Olivia down the block called a frenzy when a child rode by on a bicycle, although it almost looked to Mabel like he was trying to have a conversation. He'd better take those old bones back to Florida before he ended up on Prozac. Mabel let Tom wedge a pillow up underneath her. She let him pry her thighs a bit more apart.

Big Mama Crisp, the neighborhood children yelled whenever that big—had to be size sixteen—brown-skinned woman barreled down her driveway like a hurricane in pink sponge rollers. Best be careful, you don't know me, she warned back in a tone that promised she'd shake them if she caught them. That woman moved to this town looking for trouble, Lorraine from across the street in the beige colonial had said when Mabel ran into her down by the mailbox, and Mabel had to agree. She was looking for trouble all right, speaking her mind in front of white people.

Ruth Crisp, the winner of the biggest Florida State lottery in history, had found her dream home in Connecticut, in Greenwich and right on this street. The woman never stopped by to introduce herself; eventually it was Mabel who had gone over to the Crisp house to try and introduce her to the way things worked on Serendipity Street. She'd worn Halston, with her anniversary watch and her illegal crocodile shoes, which she figured were all right to wear although it was broad daylight since she didn't plan to step out of her Mercedes. She snuck up Rosemont and came back around so that she seemed to be coming from downtown. Ruth Crisp was sprawled in the grass, sucking on some sort of fruit. The flesh shook on the woman's legs as she came toward the car.

"Mrs. Crisp? You do know there's a streetlight fund-raising luncheon tomorrow?" Mabel'd rolled down her window and called out, although more formally than intended.

"Honey, this street's already plenty light enough for me," Mrs. Crisp answered, loud enough for a child riding by on his bicycle to hear. Mabel choked out a quick good-bye and drove home. That Saturday afternoon, Ruth Crisp had a barbecue for, as Joyce observed, about a billion negritos trucked in from God knew where. Mabel'd never seen so many plates of fried chicken. And so much potato salad they'd put it in a red mop bucket. Mabel'd had to shut the windows and turn on the air-conditioning to keep from having to smell it all day. Mabel rubbed her spine into her satin, legs high in the air. Already light enough for her, Jesus, Joseph, and Mary, too.

That woman must be out of her mind. This was Greenwich, Connecticut, not Buckswamp, Florida. A colored woman would have to be out of her mind to come barreling onto this street acting any which way. Light enough already—she must be crazy. Mabel's legs pedaled in the air and in her mind she saw the messiah rowing down a river, calling her name. That woman couldn't come to Greenwich and act any ... which ... way. Mabel grasped for the headboard. Yes, lordy lordy lordy. Yes, lordy lordy lordy. Michael, you row that damn boat, you row it all the way ashore, yes, lordy lordy.

"Work for it, Mabel, there you go," breathed Tom, voice sticky enough to reel Mabel back to her bed, where her legs were splayed embarrassingly far apart and her stretch marks were brown silk sashes crisscrossing her entire torso. Tom was up on his haunches, a squirrel burrowing into her after a nut. Mabel, mortified, swatted around for her nightdress, but Tom kept lapping. This was bound to be one more endless night unless she gave Tom what he wanted.

It was some award show—must have been the Grammys—where she first heard Donna Summer's "Love to Love You, Baby," but it was a radio deejay who she'd heard swear the chorus was made up of a woman's genuine shouts of pleasure during sex acts in a recording booth. Mabel did her thing. Tom was grinning now, triumphant, and climbing aboard. A few more minutes and she'd finally be able to get some rest.

———

One ice-cold Massachusetts day during her senior year at Wellesley, two visiting pre-frosh asked Hilary why the black womyn sat together in the dining hall, and why they all seemed to live in adjoining rooms on a certain corridor.

"The same reason white womyn do, it's safer," hissed Hilary, frightening the girls away. Nothing unusual about losing her temper before black studies class. Goddamn whiteys never could handle the truth.

Her closet housed piles of orange, green, and black scarves made of genuine kente cloth woven by her sisters in Africa, and she slung one over Mabel's old mink coat and hiked through the halls. Black girl living in Tower Court, wearing a mink over a jogging suit? Fuck you and your mama, she'd tell anybody who dared stare. White-man-built elevator took too damn long. She took the stairs, flipping her scarf in their faces the same way they flipped their nasty hair.

Fifteen minutes later, she slid into her usual seat in the black studies class. Back row, so she could keep an eye peeled to maintain her list of who said what, the same way J. Edgar did to Malcolm and Martin and the rest of the brothers who sacrificed their lives to the struggle. The veins in her high forehead pulsed as she shouted fact after fact at the solitary white chick still enrolled, cowering in a corner by the American flag in the typical, predictable whitey response.

"That piece of shit flag can't protect you anymore! Your granddaddy wrapped himself in it when he was out there lynching, your mama did too, when she torched our little girls in Birmingham!"

One lone "Well!" rang out from the back of the lecture hall, the same musical note the old men at Hilary's church in Roxbury struck during the sermon.

"My mother's from Boise, Idaho! She voted for Mondale!"

The prof, who had chickened out of wearing his dashikis to class fourth week after a white girl had complained to the college president about feeling persecuted, rapped for order. Heads kept bobbing to the rhythm Hilary was setting. She would not be silenced, not any longer.

"She's in Boise, Idaho, reaping the benefits of four hundred years of my black oppression!"

"My mom doesn't even know you!"

"No? No? Well, she'll know my name once the revolution starts, gotdammit!"

Hilary slammed out the door when class finished. She felt like smacking somebody. She snapped "White heifer" at a black sophomore who never showed up at Ethos meetings as she slipped and slid past her on a slush-covered path. Despite the cold, she could feel her insides sizzling. Stomping through the dorm, she nodded tersely, swiftly, at rare faces, dark faces. Can't take much more of these peckerwoods, somebody whispered at Hilary coming down the staircase, and she raised a hand to slap. The whiteys she pushed past might as well have been glass statues. She made it into a bathroom stall and slammed the door shut and took a seat.

She'd been tiptoeing over eggshells her entire life without even realizing it. That shit was over. Honky kitchen server drop the mashed potatoes onto her plate like she couldn't be bothered? Hold up the line until homegirl issued a formal apology to the entire black race. Suzy Q. Whitehead weeping over *Gone With the Wind* in the common room? Switch the channel to *Roots: The Next Generations* and dare those bitches to say boo. She'd been weaned on stories about honorable white people, fatherly George and honest Abe and diligent Betsy. And never one word all through school about how those same all-American heroes had snatched babies off the breasts of black mothers to sell. Not one transparency of a lynching had ever shone out from an overhead projector.

Hilary'd chanced across her first lynching one lonely day in the campus bookstore, thumbing through books while trying to decide on an elective. That slim picture book, misplaced from the black studies section, was the straw that cracked the camel's back wide open, slapping Hilary utterly awake for the first time in her life. She'd flicked through with a wet thumb until her finger dried on a page full of an assortment of clean-cut white boys and girls. It was a tight shot of a dozen Wonder Bread eaters, the same kids she'd seen in so many fifties reruns she practically could call out their names—Bif, Betty, Chipster, Moose.

Except they weren't getting their prom shot taken, they were posed in a half-moon around the black man they had just burnt on the ground like roasted game. Brotherman's mouth was stuffed with his own testicles, according to the caption. "What the hell," she'd said aloud, confused and alone in the back of the bookstore, as a clerk swept gum wrappers out of the aisle corners. She'd tucked her coat tighter around her hips and chest as the clerk swept debris into his dustpan.

For the first time ever, she felt as though she was seeing things clearly. She was going to find out everything that had gone down in the past and shout it out. It seemed the colder the weather turned, the uglier the details she learned of the crimes committed against her people. She awoke each morning with scorching headaches that unraveled down her body like black party streamers as she rose.

Four hundred black men injected with syphilis in the forties, spread through the black community, medicine stayed locked inside whiteys' laboratories, with niggerproof caps, her homegirl Danelle had whispered to Hilary under the roar of a live band as they got snacks at Schneider Student Center during a study break before midterms. They cut their proud black arms rudely past white arms and stuck their own plastic cups under the Coke dispenser. Fuck 'em, let the white girls get angry, no reason to feign sisterhood. It was Hundred Pound Head playing up on stage that night, a rock band Hilary used to follow in her white days. All night long she sat there fuming, stifling her fingers every time she caught herself strumming the air guitar. Alone now in the stall, she raked her skull with both hands, then cursed herself for the raw tracks. Today was Hair Day, time for a touch-up.

The poster that dominated Hilary's dorm-room wall was a photo of a 1930s lynching. Everybody pictured was gathering up coats and picnic baskets to go home except the brother left hanging by his neck in the tree. Cross-legged in front of it on her area rug, she uncapped a tiny bottle of Revlon lye and dribbled it into the tub of creme and set the timer for twenty minutes. She'd lost her last white so-called friend when she hung that picture. Hell no, I don't think it's a little Much, she'd told Beth. What the hell's wrong with YOU?

With the tail of a plastic comb, she spread the creme through her hair, careful not to drop any on her forehead. Beth had started crying, transparent crocodile drops careening off her jaw. She called Hilary prejudiced, which hurt less than a paper cut, wasn't even worth the effort it took to form the word. That's right, run while you can! she had boomed down the hall after Beth. Lousy little frosh milling around the corridor had all darted into their rooms to take cover. Even a couple of negroids had wondered aloud if she'd gone too far because she'd made a white girl cry. Same halfway negroes who were always foaming at the mouth for invitations to networking parties at Harvard B school, by the way. Somebody should have thought about sparing feelings four hundred years ago. Every class she went to, every hoop-rolling contest and step-singing show, every encounter with whitey, she struck a blow for the people with a loud dose of truth.

The lye was itching already, but Hilary forced it through her hair, smoothed it hard against the hairline. Her head was on fire, concentrated in the ridges she'd made when she'd scratched. She evil-eyed a lone white girl out of the bathroom and leaned against the sink as she skimmed water off her long, shiny hair. Her stomach rearranged itself into slightly looser fist as she carried her curler bag toward her homegirl Danelle's room. Three o'clock, goddammit. Time for *Oprah*.

———

Stormy was so high on clouds she almost got hit by a truck running across the street after she parked her car and stuffed dimes in the meter. The whole time she was having this intense déjà-vu experience. GERARD COLOMBIER, PHOTOGRAPHY AND PORTRAITURE read the sign, but it could have said SCHWAB'S DRUGSTORE.

Ever since the day Gerard slipped her his business card, which was this incredibly classy black card, very professional, shaped like a camera with silver print, she'd been queasy, but in an exciting way. He'd told her to drop by his studio, he was locally renowned for helping beautiful girls like her—beautiful like her!—get their start on the modeling scene. Several had gone on to highly fulfilling careers in

Manhattan, she could turn on her TV and look for the blond amnesiac on *As the World Turns* if she thought he was a liar. Something powerful, something close to earth-shattering, was about to happen to her entire existence, she could feel it. She'd like to thank her Neanderthal parents, her fourth-grade teacher with the hairy mole and droopy boobs, her dopey brother, and her ultra-naïve twin's latest incarnation, Louise Farrakhan . . . Her high heels felt as skinny as chopsticks as she stumbled inside, but in a really thrilling way.

The studio was sunny and the walls were lined with glossy head shots of all these genuinely gorgeous girls who she was almost a hundred percent positive she recognized from national commercials and ABC after-school specials. Gerard came rushing out to greet her while the bell above the door was still tinkling out a miniature version of "New York, New York," which happened to be Stormy's theme song. He literally whisked her past the waiting room full of whining little kids, straight back to this football stadium of an office with this big purple couch. Her dress was plastered to her back, she was that nervous.

"You're in college, no?" said Gerard, and Stormy took a deep breath and said yeah but just UConn and it was a pain in the beeswax, her parents guilted her into going, wasting critical years, she'd rather be getting her portfolio going. As she was talking Gerard pulled a camera from beneath his desk and lifted her chin into the light and snapped Polaroids. Stormy nearly had a heart attack waiting for the black to evaporate off the pictures.

Stunning, Gerard finally mumbled to himself, and Stormy felt the earth move. It was like God had reached a finger down and traced it around her face. Her whole life . . . her whole life . . . She was a chosen one after all. Everything was going to be okay. She felt like weeping. "Are you familiar with the Gourmet Skin Milk Company? They're casting a print ad . . ."

"Heck, yeah," said Stormy, struggling to stay calm. This was it, it was happening. As long as she didn't blow it. She sat up straighter and deepened her voice one sexy octave. "I've seen that stuff at the mall."

"How would you feel about doing an ad like this?" He pulled an eight-by-ten out of a file, a naked woman with one arm strategically blocking her boobs and a bottle of Skin Milk in front of her crotch. Okay, Stormy could manage that. That particular pose wasn't in her repertoire but any dummy could see how the girl did it, crouched kind of, propped kind of high on the foot. She'd better get her bikini line waxed. And a professional manicure/pedicure at the place with the Korean ladies.

"I could do that," said Stormy, her heartbeat racing faster than a speeding locomotive. They sold Slimfast at CVS down on the corner, she'd stop by the cash machine, then go by and pick up a few boxes.

"So you'd be into it?" he asked her, his voice squeaky with skepticism. "Some girls say they can do it and then you send them to the audition and they freeze up . . ." He licked the crevice above his beard with his pointy pink tongue.

Trembling, Stormy shrugged like an old pro. "I don't freeze up." She wondered if she needed to reassure him by letting him in on her philosophy of life, which was spelled out perfectly in last month's *Cosmo*. A girl can be a Miss Priss and miss the boat or take risks and conquer her dreams. She'd also read in a Monroe biography that Marilyn's first job was sprawling buck naked for a calendar, and look at her now, dead but still adored. She was about to assure Gerard that nudity was just an illusion when she noticed he was smiling at her like a dream come true and simultaneously handing her a wire hanger.

"You're too hot to freeze up, is that it?" he said, smiling. "A real tiger. Rrrrrr."

"Yup," she said back, as jauntily as she could manage, wondering what the heck the hanger was for. She took it, mumbling thanks.

"Go ahead and slip off your things so I can make sure you're in shape to send over to the Gourmet people." He clapped his hands and pulled out his seat to sit at his desk and seemed to forget her as he started scribbling in his appointment book.

Stormy stood there blinking. Move, she told her arms, but they just stayed flat at her sides. Obviously this was normal procedure, the hanger was RIGHT on his desk, somebody else must have JUST used it. It had to be normal procedure, the girl from the anti-smoking ads who blew her dirty breath through a piece of cheesecloth was right there among the glamour-pusses on his wall. She toed off a shoe. A guy with a

football stadium for an office wouldn't be a scam king. She
toed off the other. He was looking a little annoyed. She went
for it, lifting off her dress and draping it over the hanger's
bar. She was Mary in *Jesus Christ Superstar,* shy but sensual.

"Underwear too," said Gerard, coughing and holding out a
roll of Sucrets. If this were the famous casting couch situation, he sure as heck wouldn't be offering her Sucrets, for
chrissakes, he'd be mixing martinis. She stumbled out of her
bra and panties and stood naked, hugging her elbows, while
Gerard surveyed her, frowning up and down her body, biting
the flesh on the ball of his thumb. She waited for him to notice her lopsided breasticles but he stayed quiet about them,
a real gentleman. There were probably all sorts of putties
and makeups to camouflage such imperfections; she'd been
freaking out all these years and it probably wasn't even a big
deal. He didn't say a word, just made the okay sign. Elated,
she snapped her panties back up. He was squinting at her, and
all of a sudden he spat out a name. Josephine Baker.

Josephine Baker—his voice went dreamy—was a gal just
like her, hadn't she ever seen the pictures, he'd hung one
himself for Black History Month, those wonderful feathers,
that ripe yellow banana belt. He was out from behind his desk
now, circling her, rubbing his sandpaper palms fast like a
cricket. Europeans understood girls like Stormy, Europeans
understood that life had texture, passion, emotion. *Alors!*
Why waste her time in New York doing commercials when
she could go to Europe and become world renowned. He
stood behind her, his voice aimed down at her pumpkin butt,

which, along with her stomach, she was desperately sucking in so tight that she could feel her kidneys and liver fidgeting for space. America will never, never understand you, he whispered, sounding almost indignant, but Europe will welcome you with her arms wide open. She farted, from the pressure on her internal orangutans, and prayed on her mother's grave he wouldn't notice.

"You're unique, one of a kind," he said, facing her now and smoothing his goatee. That was Dorothy Hamill on his wall, Stormy was absolutely a hundred percent positive even though every bitch on the block had that dumb haircut. Arranging the plane ticket was her business, he continued, but he had all sorts of contact people in Madrid, then Milano and then, when she was ready, Paris. Fast as a bolt of lightning, he ran a hand through the air and left it hanging there like a starburst while Stormy gaped openmouthed at her name in lights on a European marquee.

He would shoot the portfolio because a look like hers must be done right, Kodak made some sort of new film to shoot the more olive-complexioned people. It wouldn't be cheap but if she was serious . . . he shrugged. Cash, check, or credit card. He stepped out of the room, left her alone to dress. Delighted but dazed, she kept her stomach sucked in tight even though she was all by herself.

1988

B L A C K F L I G H T

"..."

"..."

"... man oh man oh man ..."

"..."

"Damn. That geechee bitch you was bonin' befo' musta put a curse on your ass, Spade my man."

"Sheeet."

"I feel for you, my brother, but thank GAWD I'm not in your shoes. Your shit is in the pan, about to get deep-fried."

"Give me some dap on that one, my brother." Lloyd, from Idaho, got up off the bed and did a slow pimp across the area rug and banged fists with George, from Silver Springs. The air was thick with soul. Tommytwo ground his teeth. He was like, not in the mood.

"He be fucked."

"His ass be grass."

Tommytwo sure wished they'd all shut the hell up. He'd come to these guys for maybe some practical advice, maybe a little bit of sympathy, not for Shaft and Blackula to remind him that he'd flushed his life down the toilet.

"Daaaamn!" Clyde from down the hall erupted, fingers snapping so hard as he slid into the room that he could have been flicking off red ants. Tommytwo could not believe his luck. First he gets somebody pregnant—pregnant! pregnant!—and then he ends up in here with this bunch of lunchboxes when what he needed was some privacy and a Ginzu knife.

Oh God—was Dad right? Always remove yourself from a bad situation, his dad had been urging him each and every time they spoke for the past three years. Transfer. Anyplace but Morehouse, anywhere but Atlanta. He wondered what Dad would say when he found out Tommytwo was an unwed father. Dad had sworn this place would bring out the nigger in him.

"Yo, nigga, you sure she said anti-abortion?"

"Twice."

As far as Tommytwo was concerned, pregnancy was the creature from the black lagoon. When she said the word . . . oy-yoy-yoy. It came at him like a meat cleaver. PRREEG-GNNNAAANNNTT, there it still was, echoing in his hollow head. Pregnant, she'd snapped at him again when he just stood there trying to figure out what in the heck a guy was supposed to say.

Woman, don't start trippin' out on me, he'd snapped at

her, out of the blue. About the last muhfucka I need is a baby. He'd said that, in the same Superfly voice he used with the guys. To LaKisha, who knew him, the real him. She'd smacked him with her book bag, out in the middle of the quad, then run away.

If there was any slight silver lining to this fiasco, it was that now everyone on campus would know for sure that Tommytwo was nobody's piece of Spam. Oh yeah, he knew other guys had their doubts about him. He hadn't known how to play bidwist freshman year, he'd thought Don Cornelius was a Spanish explorer. But he had his own doubts about some of them. He'd seen George at Lenox Mall playing video games with white dudes in Emory sweatshirts. And he'd heard plenty of guys in bio asking for recommendations, diction white as milk. He'd heard Pinky in lab one afternoon answering to the name Burgess like a fucking puppy. Burgess. If there ever was a guy with a name whiter than Burgess would he speak now or forever hold his peace. Oh boy. Oh boy boy boy. Tommytwo was screwed.

"Yo ass be grass, my brother."

"Yo, like, could you guys please chill."

"All I was saying was you Fucked, my brother. With a capital *F.*"

Tommytwo stuffed his fists into his ears and hummed "The Star-Spangled Banner." Oh yeah, and his mom, oh man. His mom was going to keel. As for his dad, being at Morehouse was bad enough, let alone getting some girl pregnant. Let alone getting some girl named LaKisha pregnant. LaKisha was different, the real deal. She was from Detroit, down and dirty, knew guys who'd taken heroin, had gone out with a guy who'd stabbed his cousin.

"She probably planned it, yo ass ax me. Probably took her a needle and poked a hole in the rubber, you ax me. Ax her before you go marryin' her, man, just ax her." Clyde, from Alaska, was the Christopher Columbus of discovering words in black English, but had never heard of overkill.

"Marry?! Nigger, you need to trip your black ass out the window. What law says brotherman got to go that far?"

"Word! Babycake come from the screets. Her mama be pleased as punch she found a college nigga to knock her ass up."

"I said chill," said Tommytwo. There was no rubber. Under all the gold jewelry, LaKisha was an old-fashioned girl. She didn't believe in modern technology separating her Esmerelda from his Big Daddy. That was what she called it. Big Daddy. Even in front of her girlfriends.

She was one of a kind, as far as Spelman went. Your typical Spelman girl would let a guy spend his last ten bucks on a plate of spaghetti marinara, then go bounding back inside her dorm like a kangaroo, forget the kiss. Not LaKisha. She'd cook a guy a meal on a hotplate. She carried herself like Miss Universe, and he'd figured she was safe.

"How she be lookin', ya'll?"

"She fine. Spader like 'em black but fine."

"Long hair?"

"Hell naw. To the neck. Baby got a body though."

"Today she got a body. Six months from now she'll be one big fat stank ho talkin' bout where the pickles—"

"I said chill!" These assnoses could talk trash all they wanted, but they better keep LaKisha out of it, period. If they'd seen her expression, talking about going to Detroit all by herself to raise the ba . . . the ba . . . the baby. He'd taken in about half the words she'd said out there in the quad, something about having the kid underwater in a birthing pool, teaching it how to swim from day one like a tadpole. LaKisha loved the ocean. Forced him to watch *Miami Vice* on Friday nights. Popped popcorn on the hotplate. Giggled every time the tinfoil blew up like a balloon. Son, remove yourself from bad situations. Screw you, Dad. I love her.

"Yo, hand me the phone."

The guys shouted Tommytwo down. Don't call her, was he out of his mind, leave the bitch be, wait her ass out. It was beginning to get on his nerves. It was his life, his choice.

"Hands me the phone, Pinky bro. I needs to calls my girl, make sure is she be doing okay." His soul train had jumped track, the words were falling off his tongue mangled, but it was okay for once. He loved LaKisha! They were going to have a baby! Cigars, what he needed was cigars.

———

Madrid was dead the night Stormy finally agreed to go out with her boss, Juan Carlos, so it must have been a Sunday. The guy was foaming at the mouth to take her out, so she figured, what the hay. She hung around with him until closing time and it was actually quite fun, drinking shots of Manzanilla and gossiping about this one particular customer who had a job at the palace and went out with transvestites on his nights off.

After they deposited the night's money, Juan Carlos took her to this place, Dulce Vida, for drinks, and it was absolutely mellow, strings of white lights, a patio, a band. They were having this crazy conversation, half in Spanish, half in English, and she was yelling at him, yes, she swears she's black even if she doesn't look like these Africans selling their soda and their pleather belts down in the metro, and he's yelling back, *Yo no lo creo,* you're too pretty, or whatever, you'll be a famous model any day now, blah, blah, blah. Juan Carlos was all, You've got to be Brazilian, you're so beautiful. He kissed her neck and she pretended she didn't notice. There was definitely a hint of romance in the air.

He gets this great idea that they should drive to his apartment, and they end up looking at his baby pictures, and Juan Carlos gets all emotional because he hadn't spoken to his mother in ten years and there she is cuddling him as a baby in all these snapshots or whatever. But frankly Stormy was not in the mood to be anybody's psychotherapist so she starts yawning and hinting about Take Me Home. Next thing she knows, he's got this judo belt wrapped around his waist and he's flinging himself on her in the most obnoxious way imaginable. Literally jumps on her, like a monkey, it was so bizarre. And crazy as it seemed, that was it, his seduction routine. And she's all, Hey, you're my boss, remember the

American Bar, you're my boss, and hurdling over his nice white couches.

All of a sudden, he pulls this gun out of a cedar box and goes, in really fast Spanish which she somehow managed to understand probably due to an adrenaline rush, Okay, if you're not having fun I'll drive you home. He's got this maniacal look on his face, the same exact look he got that time the register was twenty mil short and the guy Antonio that used to work there showed up in new cowboy boots.

Every bone in her body was like, Catch. A. Cab. But in the first place she didn't want to upset him and have him shoot her and ruin her parents' lives. In the second, he lived by Chamartin somewhere in the boonies and it would have been two mil by cab, two mil at the very least, and that was only if brain-bone connected to tongue-bone and her Spanish came out believable enough that the driver mistook her for a South American prostitute and didn't try to give her the tourist special, a detour through Málaga. Most *morenitas* were South American prostitutes, her uptight roommates were always reminding her. Anyway, the bottom line was *dinero*. It was like, ride home with Juan Carlos or eat cheese *bocadillos* all week. So she gets in the car and he takes her straight home. *No pasa nada. Gracias a Dios.*

Then two nights later she goes out with Bliss, who's already got her book nine-tenths completed, including some headshots by this world-renowned photographer named Jean-Claude Somebody-or-Other who Bliss said was so emaciated-looking naked that she made him wear a rubber even though he was world famous, which he took as a big insult. Groaning with laughter over absolutely nothing from the time they met at Metro Bilbao, the girls shoved each other into the nearest bar, a neighborhood dive full of middle-aged men talking through clouds of smoke and a sleeping dog beneath a chair.

Every head, including the dog's, pivoted to watch them enter, they could have been on a runway. The men scooted their chairs apart and patted empty vinyl seats, and called out to the grinning bartender to pour the girls glasses of sherry from one man's native Jerez and wine from another man's hometown outside Barcelona. I love Spain, Stormy told the man whose arm was resting on her seat back, as she sipped her amber wine. The man's eyes glazed and he licked his lips and left them hanging apart. I am Spain, he said, pursing for a kiss, and Stormy patted his furry old cheek and spun away. *Adelante!*

On to the Burger King in Plaza de Espana, which was dotted with old men in olive sweaters who lifted the bun and sniffed the meat before they bit it. The girls were genuine American starlets as they ate their Whoppers, the way everyone stared. They go into the bathroom and borrow each other's eye liner and fix their bustiers and burst gloriously into the streets, talking loud English, the magic language that everyone they met had tapes of or was enrolled at an academy to learn. They strutted down the center of every plaza and every avenida, practically owning the cobbled roads. *Una cerveza por favor,* they said over and over and over.

Somewhere around midnight, there they were, Stormy and

Bliss, sipping *vodka y naranjas,* and somebody passes them *un porro* and they're toking as hard as they possibly can before they have to pass it back, and this guy Pedro, who always hung out there and who they both had desperate crushes on—partially because there was nobody else better to have a crush on—whispers something in really fast Spanish about *después. Después* meant "afterward," even Bliss caught that, and Bliss's Spanish was the same level as that of all those loser tourists who crawled around like turtles under their backpacks and didn't know how to say anything but Which way to the Prado Museum? Stormy still hadn't been to the real Prado, but she'd gotten free drinks at a bar called the Prado.

Next thing Stormy knows, it's four in the morning and she's throwing a leg over the back of Pedro's motorcycle, waving *adiós* to Bliss, who had to be dying of jealousy even though according to her she's got an early shoot. Yeah, right. If she'd had an early shoot, Stormy would have heard about it all night. They zoomed through the streets, Stormy's nails digging into Pedro's thighs, both of them screaming *Madrid Me Mata* with all their might. At some point that night, she got heaved into a swimming pool at this really cool disco, way far away. Pedro's hash was really great, except that she got this excruciating hangover, which only a day full of *cervezas* starting early the next afternoon even began to put a dent in. Like Columbus, she accidentally discovered this whole street called Moncloa, made up of one bar after the other, people spilling out on the street holding *copas* of golden *cervezas* with these big beautiful foamy white heads.

By Thursday night, Stormy was chanting to herself, I need rest. I must stay here at the *pensión*. I will plant myself in the TV room and listen to María Carmen and María José speak Spanish, no matter what. Just as she decided, Evan calls, the guy from the base in Torrejon, who all the Joes in the *pensión* think is her cousin since everyone American and black must thus therefore be automatically related. He knew about some really cool party.

So she agrees to meet him at Tierra because, shit, she barely even remembered what her room back home looked like, she was that homesick sometimes. Nobody in this *retardo* country could even pronounce her name without wincing. And her roommates here hated her guts because she was young and everyone called her a gorgeous mulatta and she didn't care about learning frigging local history because soon she was going to be famous and forget she ever knew them. And Spanish food sucked, full of olive oil. She hadn't been that homesick since her first week in Spain, when she'd ridden through Old Town with strangers in a rattly Citroën that bumped over curbs and parked on sidewalks. They stopped at bars run by ex-bullfighters who remembered every detail of each corrida memorialized on the hand-painted posters lining the stucco walls and who frowned in surprise when she suddenly burst into tears, thinking she was crying at the brutality of the sport when actually she was crying because she missed her dumbass brother.

Of course the Marías had multiple orgasms when they saw Stormy leaving to go to a club by herself at midnight. María Carmen, who happened to be a forty-year-old virgin with long black strings of hair in her armpits that she could have cut and sold, called Stormy a *puta* on her way out. Yo mama, Stormy said back.

The whole party was vibrating to the music and drinks were like two mil apiece and all these rich guys were in love with her and treating and she was tossing them back. They even offered her some cocaine in a little baggie, but screw dying of heart palpitations in a foreign country and have her parents regret the day she was born. Not to mention wrinkling prematurely.

The lights were strobe, the Spanish guys were ultra macho. Stormy threw back her neck, arched like a swan's, as she laughed. It was an adult Disneyland, this Spain, and come autumn, a train ride away, bulls would run through the streets of Pamplona. She'd wear beautiful dresses like Ava Gardner in *The Sun Also Rises* and dance at festivals and sip wine and she would glitter, inside her dark skin, standing out among the other stars. The bartender was admiring her while the men gathered round and smacked one another's backs gleefully as they taught her how to say all the best obscenities. *"Polla, no me jodas, me cago en la leche, puta, maricón ..."* She repeated the string of sounds until all the guys roared with laughter and the bartender put an icy bottle of champagne on the counter and set out new plates of peanuts. They totally did not expect her to pay.

Evan was friends with the deejay, so whenever she wanted she could climb into the booth. All three of them called each other Homey, and Jazzy George played all the best songs, like

"White Lines" and "Push It," and they nearly fell out of the booth, they were having such the ultimately fabulous time.

When she and Evan strode through on their way out, they got mobbed by star-struck Spaniards groping and pulling on their sleeves to talk about the summers they'd spent in Evanston and Des Moines and how much they loved that movie *Guess Who's Coming to Dinner.* Stormy got proposed to like fourteen times within three minutes. By the time they got out to the street, it was getting light out, and the swarms of old women in widow weeds were already armed with lashed straw mops and buckets and getting ready to wash the twisting sidewalks. They looked Stormy, in her miniskirt, up and down, shaking their heads in palpable disgust, as if Stormy gave a damn. She and Evan about died laughing. They laughed right in the old women's faces and tossed coins at them to buy real mops, twentieth-century mops like the ones you could buy in any Kmart in America, and shouted "Wasn't slavery abolished?" as they stamped footprints in the soapy water.

When Evan told her about another party at the next club a few blocks down, Stormy was all, duhhh, of course I wanna go. By then, they both had somehow acquired these red-feather Indian headdresses from someplace and they were falling all over each other hugging and trying to remember the words to that first Grandmaster Flash song, the dumb one. It was a great moment out there, bouncing along in his weird little Citroën, the warm city air sweet as a cabby's cologne. It was really what life was supposed to be like, a Pepsi commercial practically, until she notices that instead of nosing around for parking spaces, the car was speeding down a highway. Evan mumbles something about he forgot his jacket, and that's all he says. She waits for more, but his eyes were glued to the road, fat red veins etched in the whites. Whoops. Something was weird.

Next thing she knows, she's in some little village somewhere and he's managed to pin her shoulders against his waterbed. The whole room's shaking like Jell-O and she doesn't want to scream because this still could be some kind of practical joke and why get the guy kicked out of his apartment because she has a lousy sense of humor. His weiner is *al aire,* just waving in the air, not really trying to poke at her, just sort of standing there like a guard dog, stirring whenever she tried to leave.

He wouldn't let her open the front door, not for hours, and he didn't even have the manners to offer her food or water. He just kept saying I love you. I love you. I love you, in this weird monotone voice, and she was like, I love you too, but can you give me a ride back to the city. It had to be *Candid Camera,* she kept telling herself, until she heard street vendors outside the window talking about closing up their kiosks to go have lunch. About then, Evan tells her to get the fuck out.

A sleazy Spanish girl in a miniskirt, just that asshole's type, was stepping off the elevator as she left. The girl practically spat at her and Stormy practically spat right back, then all the way down in the elevator she tried to figure out why and couldn't.

So then last night, Stormy was absolutely, absolutely staying home no matter what. And then Morris, the Tunisian guy, calls. They meet at this bar called Mercurio, and it's one of those bars where everybody's making out and you could practically see the positive ions ping-ponging through the air. So next thing she knows, she and Morris, who have always had a strong flirtation going, have their tongues down each other's throats against a pole and he's following her up the steps to his long, broken-down American car.

His neighborhood was in the red-light district, real live syringes in the gutter, an old woman in a crocheted vest full of loops and no bra whatsoever perched on a car, calling out to the men going by. His apartment was awful, this one dark room with posters of *Spartacus* taped to the walls, and his underpants were dingy and he lowered them and jacked off against her leg. It was all so gross. Every time she got up to leave, he begged her to stay, pulled out an American-made remote-control car, and promised her they'd go to the park later on and play American Couple and have a great time. In the park with Morris that gray morning, watching his pink miniature Cadillac remote-control car bump into trees, was the loneliest she had ever felt in her entire life.

When she got home her clothes and skin smelled like an ashtray and somebody must have been messing with her shutters in her *pensión* room because all of a sudden they let in too much light to sleep soundly. She dreamed, in broken Spanish, of her sister calling her whitey, while children ran noisily home for lunch beneath her window. She stayed burrowed there under the blanket until the children galloped back to school again in the late afternoon. It was the first time she ever thought seriously about giving it all up and heading back home to Connecticut and becoming—gross—a math teacher, with adult acne and saggy boobs or whatever. Dedicating her life to helping others learn a bunch of useless junk. Screw that. She was going to make this shoe fit. *Adelante!*

So this morning she wakes up early and she's writing a letter home, telling Mom and Dad about the Prado Museum and the Royal Palace and the blind guy who plays flamenco music on the corner and about going to María Carmen's widowed mother's house in Toledo for the weekend, and the phone rings. Its a blast from the not-distant-enough past, Juan Carlos, her boss. He wasn't exactly apologetic but he's all, *Qué pasa,* you coming in to work today. He said she was so gorgeous she'd driven him a little bit crazy the other night. We Spaniards have hot blood, he said.

To make a long story short, he offers her a promotion, a job on a terraza he's going to part-own on La Castellana, which is pretty much a hangout for the beautiful people, much more so than the American Bar. The sort of people who jet-set all over the world hang out there, lots of models and photographers, Julio Iglesias came by a lot. She would definitely meet tons of people who could help her career. Plus, the place was already known for having the best-looking waitresses in the city and now he's thinking about having some guy from Milano design these white miniskirts that came to him in a dream.

In about five minutes, they completely bury whatever little bit of hatchet there still was, because he's actually a cool guy, and besides, the whole thing with his mom really sucked,

Stormy could have been more sympathetic, not such a bitch. She wrapped herself in a towel and hurried down the hall to the shower, hoping La Señora with her moldy, yellowed rule book from the nineteenth century didn't catch her barefoot and chase her back to her room. A stream of water dribbled over her body, warm first, then cool. She had just enough cash left under her mattress to buy textured pantyhose for her date tonight.

———

A spot on Beacon Street? A jogger passing by broke pace and tripped over his feet staring at Hilary getting ready to ring the buzzer. It had taken some searching but she'd finally found a group of brothers and sisters who were after serious change. Hardnose brothers and sisters, some still in school, others already out in the workplace like Hilary, all committed to the same mission Hilary was on: rooting out oppression. The organization, known only by the acronym FIST, was founded to attack the white supremacist footsoldiers guarding the nation's hallowed halls of government, its libraries and its police stations, its banks and its classrooms. Only blacks and browns allowed. New members read Mao and Fanon and had to be able to recite certain passages. The meetings were twice a month at the Beacon Hill apartment of Hilary's old childhood friend Ball Odell. Women each brought a dish.

"My brother."

"Sister Spader. Girl, you always look so scrum-deeliicious."

Damon, a guy she'd met at the last meeting, planted his fist on his waist and stood there in the corridor smiling and shaking his head and groaning Goddamn as she walked past him toward 7C. Damon was a true militant—the first person to use the verb "infiltrate" when they were going around the circle last time introducing themselves by the companies that signed their paychecks—but he was also a Southern man. He grew up in Alabama and that's how they were in areas with dense black populations: extremely appreciative of the Afrikan female figure. Then had to live in Amerikkka by the white man's sterile rules and that's what tonight was all about, breaking free from all those invisible chains.

Hilary Spader was no castrator. She dropped her hips side to side as she walked. She actually felt ridiculous, but she knew that was only because she herself had grown up steeped in the white man's sludge, alienated from her true black cultural heritage. She was here tonight to serve her brothers and sisters in whatever way she could. *Non ministrari, sed ministrare,* just like she'd learned in college.

"Hey, girl!"

"Hey there, sugar!" Claudia, the pregnant woman she recognized from last month, pulled open the door. Hilary would never have expected a snot-nosed jerk from Hamden like Ball Odell to have grown into a whiz-kid stockbroker with an apartment on Beacon Hill with leather couches and an entire wall full of electronic equipment. There was a framed Huey Newton poster propped against a wall, and somebody had lit incense. Although the streams of smoke were drifting out the window, it lent the room a vibe like something big was about to happen, like any minute the Symbionese Liberation Army would be stepping in, big, black, and proud, berets tipped just

so, ready to turn this white-man honkytonk of a country upside down and inside out.

"Full house tonight," said Hilary, eyes darting to find familiar faces. She still felt a bit conspicuous being militant in
public, even after all that time being the blackest of the black
at Wellesley. She saw one friend, Paulie, from Brandeis.
Checking out some kid moping in the corner, some bike messenger. Better keep that stuff under wraps, these phobes
would kick his ass out of here in a minute. Ball, of course,
Ball Odell. Good old Ball Odell from Hamden. She knew a
secret about him too. Something that had made his eyes get
big as eight balls when they first bumped into each other after
all these years, down at Government Center. She'd been
wearing her white drag that day, pink blouse and gray flannel
skirt, coming from her teaching job, but that wasn't why he'd
waited until they'd ordered lemonades at a booth near Durgin
Park before he'd mentioned FIST and invited her to the next
meeting. There was another reason.

"Brother be taking his shit SERious," she covered when
Mariah caught her staring at Ball's crotch. This revolution
will not devolve into a singles' scene, that had been Mariah's
very special little contribution last time when they went
around the circle. She didn't have to introduce herself, not
Mariah. Everybody knew Mariah. Mariah was down. Mariah
went to work in braids and a gold Egyptian-print fez, Mariah
told stories about the shade of red her boss had turned when
she told him Jesus was a black man and broke it down by pas-
sage, woolly hair and what have you.

According to that sister over there in the tight mudcloth

print dress, Mariah even had a Panther aunt who had given birth to a baby in jail back in the heyday. This was Mariah's revolution in a way, since it was her idea to start meeting after those honky punks ran the brother into the street and killed him. Get some brothers who're ready for some action, that was her recruiting call, and word was spreading around Boston like greasefire. One brother even took a helicopter in from Martha's Vineyard to be here tonight, somebody whispered to Hilary. And that sister in the mudcloth dress two sizes too small is already on him like white on rice. Rest of us don't stand a chance.

"Ya'll little young ones do not want to cross Mariah. Nuh-unh. Better cross your heart and hope to die, you mess with Mariah," said Franklin as he stabbed a drink into the table beside Hilary. Franklin worked at IBM by day and was a bit older than the rest of them, late twenties, maybe even thirty. He kept his afro long enough that it was an obvious attempt, a drunk's attempt, to make a statement to the white world. The problem with that afro was, the spot on the middle where it was thinning grew about a thumbsbreadth longer than the rest of his hair. It looked incredibly bizarre, like a cork in a jug. If the white boys at IBM were anything like the white boys she grew up with, they laughed themselves silly over that plug of hair. He'd probably be the one Hilary'd end up hooking up with, knowing her bad luck. It was the Wellesley curse, interminable chastity. She hadn't even had the threat of a date in six lousy months.

Franklin could have chosen about eight different women to warn about the wrath of Mariah, but he'd homed in on Hilary.

She hated that shit. You grow up in a white neighborhood, so you automatically have a white phase and it follows you around like skunk rot for the rest of your life. No matter what town you live in, no matter how militant your friends, no matter how many sets of kente-cloth place mats you own, you're always on the margin, people always suspecting you're a Benedict Arnold.

The truth was Hilary was actually closer to being Mata Hari. She knew all about Them. She'd taken quaaludes and piano lessons, simultaneously, with the children of CEOs and senators, she'd hurled bottles out of limousine windows on senior night and shouted Our Class Rules! out of the moon-roof with an abandon that only white kids were supposed to experience in this land of the free.

She'd . . . she'd laughed alongside them at Jesse Jackson on the evening news when they showed clips of him hugging Jewish leaders after the whole Hymie thing, as if anybody really believed all was forgiven. Nope, her mouth had said, many, many times. I don't think King deserves a holiday, it wasn't like he was president of the United States or anything. Deep down inside, her stomach had ground like a butter churn, each and every time. I like blue and green and pink and purple people all the same, she practiced saying in her best white-girl voice beneath the roar of Public Enemy in Ball's living room, because the time when the revolution would need her special services was chugging round the corner, she could hear it.

"Say what?" said Mariah, and her eyes took a detour as she turned to Hilary, scooting right up to Hilary's hairline, then back to sidelong and suspicious. Everything snapped into place that fast. Last meeting, putting the food away afterward, somebody'd asked Hilary where she got her hair done. Without thinking, she'd told them, Lord and Taylor. Nothing to be ashamed about, the brother who relaxed it was a one hundred percent down brother, down to the ground, but by the time she got a chance to explain that, Mariah was already bopping her head in slow but steady motion, signifying she already got the picture, Lord and Taylor, mmm-hmmm, figures. Now that Hilary saw Mariah was giving her the deep-freeze on the basis of her patronizing an establishment hair salon, she'd simply wipe her record clean after the meeting by explaining that the blue-haired ladies got their wash-and-sets in an entirely separate room. Not that anybody had died and appointed Mariah Nubian queen just because she drove to a girl in Roxbury to get her braids done, but there was no reason to voluntarily sic an angry Afrikan woman on oneself.

"Turn down the music and let's get started, ya'll," said Brandon from L.A., who was fwiner than fwine tonight in his tight-as-Saran-Wrap Levi 501s. Last time in the kitchen, a fly on the wall would have thought those blue jeans, inseams taut as wire, were demand number one on the Ten-Point Platform. He did indeed have a girlfriend, Ruthie had given the update on that situation. A light-skinned sister, at least as light as the beige-ish rubber drain rack they were setting the dishes in but not as light as the maple floorboards, said Ruthie, and everyone's eyes had ricocheted around the kitchen. Ruthie wasn't certain about the hair since homegirl had a hat on but she looked like the type to have something curly going on up under there. She thought she was cute, Ruthie could tell by the way she'd shimmied her cheek all up for him to kiss. There in the kitchen, the cleanup committee had all cooed at one another and tilted cheeks toward one another, until Mariah came billowing back across the linoleum in her skirts, with a crusty bowl of baked beans they'd forgotten.

"Come on now, ya'll, Brother spoke the word, we're already getting a late start." Mariah barged into groups wedged in the windowseats, clapping her hands, staring down the few brave enough to keep conversating.

"Bitch like that'll eat you alive," Franklin slurred into Hilary's ear as she dropped down onto a pillow up near the front, wetting her ear. Grossed her out completely. There was a power struggle going on over by the CD player—old Motown from the sixties or keep on Public Enemy?—and another one over which brothers stood and which ones sat on speakers. Hilary was starting to get itchy. They hadn't gotten a thing accomplished at the other meeting Hilary had come to last month, but Claudia had promised the three-hour-long bitch, moan, and dine session was a rare occurrence.

"Before we commence, Brother Brandon, let me just relate the incident that occurred yesterday afternoon in broad daylight at approximately one P.M.," said Sali Muhammad, whose name used to be Arthur Fuller until he quit his junior-exec job at Digital and went independent as a consultant. "This man beside me"—he patted the bike messenger on the back—"was taking a stroll down the street, minding his own business."

"His own damn business," said Ball, who still hadn't evolved past that really obnoxious way of talking he'd had as a kid, like somebody had died and elected him the next Albert Einstein. Mommy gave me jelly beans and jelly beans are made of gelatin! Ha, ha, h-ha, ha.

"Policeman rolls up beside him, tells him to show some identification."

"Out of the blue?"

"Out of the clear blue sky. And Brotherman ain't got no ID! Brother left his wallet on the kitchen table that morning, he was on his way back home to get it."

"Ain't had a damn thing on him, not even a sheet of company letterhead." That was Ball again. My pumpkin's a jack-o'-lantern 'cause it's got a candle, ha ha, ha ha.

"Pigs will capitalize on no ID every time," sniffed Mariah, eyes rolling to high heaven. Word up, said a sister in the back of the room.

"Threw my man up against the squad car, nearly tore the chin off his face. Shoved my man's arms behind him like a damn chicken wing." The bike messenger pulled out an Ace-bandaged wrist and let it wag like a flag on a windless day.

There was fire in the brother's eye when he lifted his head and showed the white pad of bandage taped beneath his jaw, and all of a sudden, Hilary felt it burning her too. Fucking lynch mobs. What black folks needed to do was get together and start rooting out these people one by one—and not just the so-called bad apples. Black people needed to make some connections with Central America, get ahold of some weaponry, some bayonets. She pictured herself in a jungle, a length of steel pressed into whitey's neck, muddy sweat curling down her arms into her camouflage shirt, spitting out the words I don't care if your best friend is black. Hilary threw a hand high to speak her piece but Brandon didn't see it.

"These people are getting away with far too much shit," shouted Sali Muhammad.

"That's why we're here," called out somebody else. "This damn racist Boston dealt out about all the shit I'm willing to wade through."

"We, my brother. We. We're all in this together. The other day I was at the grocery store, trying to buy my baby some milk."

"Tell it, brother."

"A quart of damn milk. Was that too much to ask without one of these bigots messing with me?"

"Talk to me, my brother," sang out Mariah, hitting all the right notes.

"You know how they got all the racks of magazines by the checkout? Brother who raped that white woman plastered on all the covers this week?"

"Anybody ain't seen that ain't been out the house." Know-it-all Ball. Na-nanny-na-na. I've-got-a-jigsaw.

"White woman customer looked at me, then at the magazine. Me, the magazine. Me. Magazine. Dropped her English muffins right on the belt and ran out the store. Security guard—and thank Allah he was a brother or my ass might be in jail today—told me that shit happens all the time."

"It's getting wild out there," spat out Claudia, weeble-wobbling in from the kitchen with a bowl of greens. "I sure don't want my baby boy growing up in this mess. Greens are hot, ya'll come on."

"Next thing we'll look up, they'll be passing Jim Crow laws, so we better get this meeting started," called out Hilary. Number one, Al Green got on her nerves with all that wailing, and number two, CP time was holding up the revolution. People were eyeballing that bowl of greens and the chicken on a platter as if the plenary meeting was nothing but the after-dinner entertainment.

About ten seconds later she was wishing she'd been born without a mouth. Sali Muhammad was looking at her like she had Idiot spelled out in Christmas lights across her forehead, as was everybody else in the room. Mariah was leaning across somebody to elbow a guy in the ribs.

"Let me tell you something, baby girl. Ain't nobody no time, no where, no way, gonna pass no Jim Crow law on me," said Brandon. "Let them try."

"I got this here if somebody starts talking about the back of some bus." Ball Odell, of all people, had the nerve to pat his fly.

"You just recently graduated from college, right?" said Brandon, squinting over heads to see Hilary. "Sweetheart, there's one thing you need to know about me before this meeting goes any further." He smiled around the room as he spoke, big white healthy black-man's teeth. "White man tell me not to drink out his water fountain, you know where I'm at? Somebody help little sister out here."

Hilary felt like the world champion of morons. She grinned, tried to hold it steady. Her head felt like a giant grinning thing on a stick.

"Tell her, my man. You know my man Odell, don't you.

This my man right here. Go on, spread the word to baby sister. Where I'm gonna be?"

"At the fountain," said Ball. At the fountain, at the fountain, on a mountain at the fountain. Damon from Alabama, perched on one of the coveted speaker seats, went rolling off to slap hands with Franklin, who was bleary-eyed by this point across the room, laughing so hard his drunken knees were buckling. The whole room was in an uproar, people falling backward off pillows, laughing at Hilary.

"Thanks, BALL," said Hilary. The room quieted lightning fast, as if somebody'd kicked the master volume.

"Or don't people call you that anymore? Well, BALL?"

". . . Maybe we'd better all chill and have some of this delicious food Sister Claudia came by early to fix—"

"First I want BALL to answer my question, all right, BALL? Or did you GROW out of that nickname? Well, BALL?"

Ball was squirming on a speaker in a way that only a guy with missing pieces could do, what with all those sharp corners. And Hilary pointed that out into the still air in her loudest, cruelest voice. Ball quit twitching.

Next thing Hilary knew, she was on the small end of the peephole, whispering to Claudia that yes, she understood, she'd disrespected the brother, it was best that she leave for now, keep in touch. Plates and silverware clinked from inside the apartment as Claudia pressed the door closed.

1989

WHITEFLIGHT

Mabel certainly was Queen Bee lately. She'd had more visitors this week than she'd had in ten years. Here came Lorraine up the walk at ten A.M., carrying an Entenmann's ring Danish and wearing a look of concern. Well, she could go right back home, Mabel had already heard the news: Ruth Crisp had been spotted up on a ladder early this morning, inspecting the roof of the Bonner house. Which added fuel to the rumor that there'd been a secret deal struck between Ruth Crisp and Norman Bonner. She wanted a second home on the same street, he needed cash to move to California, according to the mailman. Serendipity Street was crackling with electricity.

"Heard the news already?" called Lorraine from halfway up the walk, and Mabel smiled and waved.

"You sure you've heard the very latest?" called Lorraine, shaking the Entenmann's box like a bone for a puppy, and Mabel waved again as she shut the door.

Ruth Crisp was going to do it. Hair as nappy as a burr patch, legs fat as a bull's, but she was going to buy the Bonner house. Nose flat as a skillet, arms black as blood sausage, but she was about to own two pieces of property on Serendipity Street. And the rest of these neighbors were about to lose their minds.

Mabel had never seen white folk so paranoid. The prematurely bald fellow down the street had stayed home from work today, and it was the first time Mabel had ever seen him riding a lawnmower. Couldn't even operate it. His eye stayed trained on Ruth Crisp's door. Ruth Crisp had been seen walking down to the Bonner house twice today already, and walking back grinning like a banshee both times, according to the old diva next door, who usually wouldn't even tell Mabel hello. If Mabel wasn't hopping up to answer the door, she was peeking out the window. Something was on the verge of explosion, Mabel could feel it in her bones.

Norman Bonner had beat his wife until her kidneys failed, and now he was a merry widower fixing to move to California. That was who they should have been watching. Ruth Crisp might be an uncouth mess, but at least she didn't beat folk up at night. She'd hollered at a Girl Scout selling cookies door-to-door once, true, but Mabel bet her bottom dollar there was more to that story than met the eye.

"It's just the underhandedness of the situation that bothers me, the sneaky way Norm's going about it," lied Ginny Riggs over coffee around noon, scanning Mabel's eyes for reaction.

They were taking Mabel for a fool. The underhandedness,

Mabel's behind. Grown people, drinking somebody's coffee and lying. Mabel knew exactly what was going on: Ginny Riggs was trying to spark her indignation. Mabel was supposed to get hot and bothered enough to volunteer to have a word with Ruth Crisp. Ruth Crisp went barefoot until November, but somehow she and Mabel had so much in common they could have an intimate chat about buying property although they'd barely ever said boo to one another. Mabel smiled and said Oh Really and poured coffee and cut Danish and saw no evil, heard no evil. Ginny Riggs chewed off every last fingernail, then got up and left.

Norm Bonner raised his kids in Greenwich schools, played golf all those years at the local club, and, let's face facts, Bev Potemkin said out of the side of her mouth when she dropped by around three, killed his wife in Greenwich. If he had financial problems, well, he had plenty of friends at the bank who could arrange some sort of low-interest loan. How does it feel getting slapped in the face, Mabel, because this was really a slap in all our faces from good old Norm. Dumping the house for less than market value and bringing everybody else's property values down with it while he ran off to California. Ruth Crisp might be offering him cash money, but he owed this community a lot more than a knife in the back, didn't Mabel agree?

"Hmm," said Mabel, taking a bite of Bev's cheesecake and dotting her lip with a napkin. Ruth Crisp had told the mailman she had twelve teenage nephews who loved white girls, so she needed space to spread out. Mabel stifled a giggle every time she thought about it. Ruth Crisp was out of her mind. The woman was absolutely insane, but she had a vault of cash money. The pretty niece who'd inherited the Georgian on the corner came by about three-thirty and sat in Mabel's kitchen chain-smoking and had the righteous tone of a door-to-door savior, which put Mabel a bit on edge. Everyone who'd been coming by had the same little bit to say, nothing too original.

The fact is, Norman Bonner is on a power trip, said Becka Rainier when she stopped over at four. Mabel could sense Becka would rather be home in bed today. Poor Becka was coming unglued because her boyfriend, Felipe, had found some rich Argentinian woman with breast implants and a yacht. Norm's on the same power trip that Chas is and that BASTARD Felipe, spat Becka, and Mabel reached out and held her hand and patted it and felt tears pool in her own eyes. Mabel knew so much about Felipe she almost felt he'd made a fool out of her too, especially after having seen Becka's leopard-print merry widow set. It's nothing but reverse discrimination, Becka sniffed when she had pulled herself together somewhat, and Mabel gently shook her head no. It wasn't time for that part yet.

You know me, I'm completely color-blind, Lorraine from across the street told Mabel, although all Mabel knew for certain was that she had a lawn jockey painted white. You know me, it could be the Rockefellers or Gettys, but the bottom line is, nobody needs to own more than one house per black—per block. Helen Hurd dropped by at dusk. There were so many young couples trying to get into Greenwich these days, said Helen. You remember my Freddy, well he's got a fiancée now and they're house-hunting, and that's just one example. And if every young couple didn't get their fair shot at buying a house and raising their kids in a sought-after neighborhood like this, if every fish in the sea didn't have the same chance to snap at the very same bait, that was simply a case of—

"Reverse discrimination," said Mabel and Helen simultaneously. Helen hummed and nodded, watching Mabel closely. Mabel fought to keep a straight face. It was almost an amusing situation to be in.

———

"Ya'll husban'!"

"Excuse me, Royetta?"

"It's ya'll husban' on the phone, soun' lak he want somethin' special!"

Mabel never should have hired a white woman, especially not one with an accent as contagious as Rocky Mountain fever. She picked up the phone.

"Hello, honey, I'll be late tonight. I'm meeting some of the fellows at the club," Tom said.

"Well, I'll see you later then. I had a whole stream of company today, and now I'm worn out."

"Mabel?"

"Yes, dear?"

"I'd like you to do something for me before you sit down to relax."

"I already sent Royetta to get that dry cleaning this afternoon. They were able to fix that zipper on your robe, but maybe it's about time to buy a new one."

"It's bad luck to buy a new robe before they announce the appointment." Tom's voice dropped to a whisper. "The first black state supreme court justice, we wouldn't want to jinx it, now would we. Which reminds me, Mabel sweetheart, I want you to take a walk."

"Take a walk?"

"I know you're tired, honey. Just a little walk. Over to the Crisp house. Some of the fellows have been trying to get a message to Ruth Crisp, but she doesn't seem to want to listen to anyone. Just try strolling over, say hello, find out how she's doing."

"What? Tom?"

"You might mention, you know, if it feels right, that Don Mulhoney down at the bank is an excellent contact person. Might want to mention he's Jewish, even though the name is Irish. Tell her a mortgage makes a heck of a lot more sense than buying a home for cash. Tell her you'd never pay out that much cash at once, no matter how much money you had."

"Tom!"

"Mabel." Tom's voice grew grave. "Listen to me. We're there. We're not almost there, we're there. Now I want you to Take A Walk, Down The Street. To keep us there."

"Tom? Tom?"

"Do it, sweetheart. Do it for us."

Tom hung up the phone and stared at the wall of his chamber. It was Joe's bright idea to try sending Mabel, and Don Mulhoney said he'd let the Crisp woman fill out some paperwork at the bank, make it look good, give them some stall time to find another buyer or to pull the money together among themselves. No chance of Mabel working things out before tomorrow, when the money was to be exchanged, it was far too late, but they might as well give it a shot, if only to show everyone was pulling for the same team.

The minute he got this near-disaster straightened out, he'd get rid of that maid Royetta. He'd told Mabel long ago to hire colored women, the darker the better, and he'd never amended that. He shouldn't have let her get away with the one Puerto Rican, that was where he'd made his mistake. Royetta answering the door and running to get Mabel was far too much of an optical illusion, if only for the UPS men and Jehovah's Witnesses. Rocked the boat. And rocking the boat at this point could be extremely dangerous.

———————

Movie title, four words. Third word must be "little." Buy a vowel, idiot. Nobody wants to hear about your daughter back in Youngstown needing money for a wedding, just buy a vowel. *Come Back, Little Sheba?* What in the world movie was that? The truth of the matter was, Mabel didn't think those people ought to own two houses on this street either. So there. She thought they ought to be more than satisfied with one house in Greenwich. That was more than the vast majority of negroes in this country had.

Mabel went to the hall bathroom and spent a few minutes rubbing on plum rouge, then found an old bottle of Fiorinal she'd forgotten inside a cylinder of toilet paper, and took the last three stuck to the bottom, to calm her nerves.

She was going to walk over to the Crisp house and she was going to do her little duty. The last thing this street needed was a bunch of unemployed Florida hicks flying here first-class to spook the girls in the cheese shop, and chase everybody out to upstate New York. Don Mulhoney, she told herself as she pulled a hat down tight on her neck and temples. Jewish although the name is Irish, Jewish although the name is Irish.

All those negroes back home would have a field day if they knew about Tom's plan. Jumped right into the white man's pocket, she could practically hear them gloat, as pleased as if they'd hit the number. Dove in headfirst, she could hear Old Man Apron shout.

But it wasn't that simple. Mabel was the Turner girl from Madison Street. Her Daddy worked thirty years as a janitor in the stockyard right alongside everybody else. And she didn't want that woman's twelve nephews living on this street either. So there. Pulling white girls' hair, shooting off firecrackers, giving these cops a reason to wake up early in the mornings. Probably start selling these white children crack cocaine and angel dust too, or whatever this week's worst drug was.

White man's pocket, nothing. Common sense, that's what that was, cold hard percentages, she'd read it in *Time* magazine just yesterday, some new percentage about the number of negroes in jail, with an inset picture of Congressman Kwesi Muhsomething saying it wasn't just the blacks destroying America, mouth wide open as if he were saying something new. The last thing she needed was cops perpetually in her yard, ringing her doorbell, wanting to know if some fourteen-year-old who'd just gangbanged somebody belonged to her. The Spader children were doing fine, one down South in college, one teaching third grade in Boston, and the last in Madrid, Spain, studying art. Mabel'd done her job and done it well, thank you very much, Officer.

Now if only Mabel could convince herself to turn off the TV and go up the street and knock on that woman's door.

Instead she took her special foot bucket out from beneath the sink and ran scalding hot water in it. She'd sit here in the living room and have a glass of brandy and soak her feet first, give herself a pedicure. The Lord had given her Daddy's bad feet, she was finding that out the older she got. Darn. Some new bunion even.

She flipped the channel. Channel nine had colored folk on, white folks' favorite kind, African babies with flies buzzing in their ears and eyes. She tested the steaming water with her toe. White children running through a field singing, Mabel got so tired of that. White woman acting prissy in some shampoo commercial, Mabel could live without that too. A spot in the back of somebody's office, but at least they had him up there typing and not just playing the delivery boy. White woman getting raped on the cable channel by a Hispanic, but at least a white Hispanic. Spot in that beer commercial, trying his best to look excited although he was the only fellow without a date. Bright-complected enough to pass for Portuguese, too.

Mabel scraped at the skin on the underside of her toe with her cuticle pusher, and she paused to marvel at the fact that at some point she'd become her Daddy: pointing out the negroes on television while she picked her toes. She could almost hear him, keeping a measure of white folk's evolution by the shows they broadcast. Climbing into the white man's pocket, she could practically hear Daddy's voice say, each syllable ringing in the living room for long moments afterward.

Wait a minute. That *was* Daddy. She stopped picking at her toes. She'd actually heard her father's voice, here, in Greenwich, in her living room. Uh-oh, she thought, because Daddy'd been dead for years. She blinked and looked around, even dried her feet and stepped two steps down the hall, but saw nothing but ceilings and walls in the fading light of a summertime dusk.

Sister Mercy used to swear she heard spirits. Woman used to swear she was sitting in her regular pew, barely even paying attention to the sermon, the day Jesus spoke her name. And after that for the rest of her life, the woman found a way to wedge Jesus into every sentence, every sneeze, every yawn. No, prayed Mabel, feet dropping in the bucket. No, no, please. Don't make me a born-again.

Ma too? Yes, that had to be Ma: Mabel Agnes Turner, you got a white girl washing your dirty drawers and you ain't called to tell nobody? You crazy? Hard as I slaved for those people all my life?

"Ma?" said Mabel, ducking her head as if from flying bats. Ma was dead! But she could hear them, there were definitely people in this living room. "Ma? Ma, how'd you get in here?"

There on your fine sofa about to do what? You about to walk over to that Crisp woman's house and do what? Girl, you better start doing some explaining before I have to find my switch.

Mabel sat on her living-room sofa, feet boiling in the bucket. Caught in a house of spirits, yet as sane as she'd ever been. *Wheel of Fortune* was still on the television, Vanna White was turning letters. Mabel took a sip of brandy. She was sitting on her Ethan Allen sofa. The sofa that her husband, who had never let her work a day in their married life, had bought her for their twenty-fifth anniversary.

"Ma, can you see me? Can you see me?" Mabel asked softly, sitting up straighter. If she wasn't losing her mind, and Ma and Daddy were actually somehow here in the room, well then Mabel would like to hear what they thought of all this. "Ma? See this couch, it's snow white, but I don't bother to cover it with plastic. I let the man come clean it. Ma?"

No carpet, but she could have had it if she wanted, she could walk out to the three-car garage and get her brand-new (bought new) Mercedes-Benz right now and drive down to that store with the gold lettering on the window and pick out the thickest, most cushiony shag carpet they made. And she could have a man in to install it tomorrow, a white man. Except—He covered all that beautiful hardwood? You must have really broken his heart, she'd once overheard Gabby McDonough tell her sister Libby on the phone, and Mabel'd made her decision to live with the wood floors.

Ma was ignoring her, Mabel could tell somehow. Ma seemed to have crawled right up inside Mabel's mind now like a poltergeist, brushing aside everything Mabel was trying to tell her, and reading text right off the ridges of her brain. And it seemed Daddy was beside Ma, chewing snuff and trying to match Mabel's life to the pictures in Ma's *Jet*. Every few seconds, Ma piped up with bewildered questions: How had Mabel Agnes come to this intersection? How had Mabel come to be sitting on a snow-white sofa, sipping Grand Marnier brandy with her feet in a special bucket, with a husband so high up on the totem pole he could have her traffic tickets fixed, and a girl to wash her panties, and a white girl at that. And how, at the very same time, could she be about to walk over to the only other colored woman's house for the first time—

The first time ever? Ma interrupted her own question. That don't make no sense neither, Mabel Agnes, said Ma, and Mabel could feel her mind being scanned from a whole different angle and it felt like a shot of icy wind. Lord but she hoped Ma wouldn't ask her about Ruth Crisp's barbecues. If Mabel'd known there was a possibility she'd have to explain the details of her life to her mother one day . . . Horrified, she saw herself locking her bedroom door and quietly winding open a window, then sniffing barbecue-flavored air for all she was worth.

"Ruth Crisp stands barefoot on her curb, Ma, and she sucks on neckbones in front of white folk," Mabel said indignantly, to try and derail Ma while she got her bearings. It seemed to work. "She cussed a child selling Girl Scout cookies," Mabel continued, in as accusatory a voice as she could muster, and that seemed to stop Ma for another long moment.

"Who yawl in heah talkin' to?" said Royetta, poking her head in.

"Privacy," snapped Mabel, and she hated being rude, but that girl thrived on controversy.

Mabel Agnes just yelled at that white woman, Mabel could hear Ma telling Daddy. Paw, you see that? It must be the year two thousand.

Told her to git out like it was a dog, said Daddy, sounding deeply ashamed. Just come on home, Mabel could sense him saying.

"But Daddy, I can't do that . . ." she started to say, then realized her ears had quit ringing.

And you gone have to run that wall-to-wall carpet business by me again the next time, said Ma, her voice hitting deeper notes as it faded. You lost me on that wall-to—

Mabel sat there on her couch for hours, shaken and annoyed. Eventually she decided that she was not insane and that no, she had not experienced a born-again conversion. Helen Hurd had told Becka Rainier she'd seen a ghost once, and if even a white woman could see a ghost, Mabel could see a ghost. But

Mabel made a promise to herself to never, not ever again, dip her feet so suddenly into a bucket of nearly boiling water, not in a house that kept a chill even in summer. And no more Fiorinal, not ever.

When Tom came home, she sat with him while he drank a gin and tonic, took a sip herself. They both sat there silent until a certain moment came, the moment when that Ruth Crisp business hung in the air above them like a piece of sculpture. Mabel gave a little nod when the moment came, a teeny tiny nod, and if he took it to mean something it didn't, so be it. He held her hand and kissed her palm and pressed it against his cheek and eyelid.

Johnny Carson had an entire array of guests that night that Mabel had never heard of. She watched Tom in the blue light of the television as he sank into a deeper sleep. He'd always been a fitful sleeper, looked like he was fighting demons. She watched him for a while, watched him toss like he always did.

Yes, she'd better start going back to her little Vietnamese woman for her pedicures.

Only the devil himself knew what went on inside of Tom Spader's head while he slept. He awoke clammy this morning, before dawn, and endured the usual vivid, lightning flash of terror. Dreams were Tom's only real difficulty, the weak link. Memories could be suppressed at will, but he had not yet mastered dreams.

He said his morning prayers, giving thanks for Mabel and

the children. Morehouse. His first clear thought was always Morehouse, and what was to be done. Was the boy bent on sabotaging his entire life? Or was he merely hopelessly naïve, caught up in some urban fantasy, unwilling to believe that rubbing shoulders with a bunch of eager colored boys was useless indulgence even for a day, never mind for four years. Tom had told that boy a thousand times: Every moment counts. Obviously he had never listened.

Mabel, sweet dear Mabel, was less a blessing than a prize. He'd won her, the prettiest girl in town. This morning he allowed himself several long glimpses of Mabel and himself as youngsters in love, kissing shyly by the river, as he dressed quietly in the dark. He laced his shoes and a memory, a bad one, managed to slip in through the cracked door within his mind, and lance at him like a knife. He slammed the door, convinced, as he often was, that his carefully cultivated ability to suppress memory was his only true weapon against his own complete destruction.

Destruction. Destruction. He had a breakfast appointment with Norman Bonner, speaking of destruction. Joe Klein would be there as well. The agenda was the investigation of possibilities, the development of plans, the locating of loopholes. According to Joe, that goddamn moron Norm was frantic over what he'd gone and done. Of course, by the time they met, the need for loopholes would have dissipated, the mess cleaned up. They'd clink their Bloody Marys, they'd set up a golf date, they'd not mention Norm's late wife, Anne Marie, or the garrulous Crisp woman, or even the house. If you can't stand the heat, implode, that was fine with Tom. He'd be there to clean it up. Tom would be right there, broom in one hand, moving closer to the source.

He'd greased the back-door hinges yesterday; still, a high screech pierced the night air: an error, but not critical. He paused for a moment, waited, listened, before going to retrieve a hidden plastic container. The moon's dappling the water, Mabel had told him the night he'd proposed. He allowed himself a brief moment's reflection of the lovely mound of brown lips, the hills and valleys of nearly black skin draped with a thin cotton dress. The journey had been arduous, but she'd held his hand throughout. He was a lucky, lucky man. A truly happy man.

He heard the *shush* of liquid inside the jug as he moved down the driveway. Mabel as a young girl, himself as a gaunt, terrified boy, slipped behind the door in his mind, which automatically locked. His mind remained emptied of all but the present as he stepped off the curb into the street. An enormous love coursed through him, a love as concrete as physical pain.

The Vietnam vets who faced his bench, those were the few men in this world whose minds he absolutely comprehended. Ducking from bombs even in his courtroom, dead sure of the game being played.

The other fellows, the other judges and lawyers, his colleagues, were a murkier deal. Trained to swear there was no game. There was merely Life, which consisted of twin elements, the accumulation of money and of power. Blessed not with logic, but with blinders, and ground troops. Rarely slipping, not those at the very highest plateau. Tom's work was to be present during the slips, to reassure, to clean up. To gain ground.

The other, the sloppier regiment was even more inscrutable in some ways. Kill ... one another? And then call him Brother in his own courtroom? What was the purpose, what was the plan? Brother, they called him, and then set their arms akimbo and glared at Tom through the tunnels of white men who held their pathetic black lives in their hands. Got a live one for you, he'd lean over and tell Jessel, just loud enough for everybody to hear, including the dumb coon. He'd make a show of it. Jessel would give an extra jangle of the keys and a fat wink.

The waste, too, was incomprehensible. The grimaces, the pendants made from someone's Mercedes (somebody's in this courtroom undoubtedly, you dumb porch monkey) car emblem. The energy spent on maintaining a jaw consistently slack, an eye dull, a sentence incomprehensible. The wasted murders. Tom felt such a weariness when bleary-eyed defendants came crawling into his courthouse blaming everything from the corpse in their kitchen to the corn on their knuckle on crack. At those times, he almost wondered if it was worth it to go on. What kind of S.O.B. blamed the havoc he wreaked on crack. Crack. They came to his courthouse by the dozens, letting public defenders read their lives off the rap sheet, with nothing better to say for themselves than that the crack made them do it, standing there as silently as a coon done singing his tune. A man must walk tall when he wreaked havoc, or else leave havoc alone.

Tom cradled the jug of gasoline as he crossed the shadowy street toward the catty-corner house. Damned numbskulls could rot in hell for all he cared. The day he plunged into a raging river to keep a nigger out of jail, a nigger too dumb to even figure out the most basic rules of the game, would be the same day hell froze.

These Crisps were a case in point. Thirteen million dollars handed to them on a platter, and what did they do? Did they keep it quiet, keep their mouths shut, seek advice? Or did they mosey onto any random street like moose into a tea party, pick out whichever house had cable hookup and a picnic table and invite half the black population of the state of Florida to come visit. Did they throw barbecues, trying to prove some sort of simplistic point? They should have shushed, stayed quiet. That's what to do.

The gasoline sloshed crazily. Eyes on his back, always. Tom had tried to instill that message in his son. They weren't among the throng. They were outlined in glitter on maps they would never see and circled in photographs that they would not remember had ever been snapped. The boy must be polite. He must do well in school. He must dress neatly, bathe regularly, keep elbows well below the tabletop. He had no choice. The boy must learn from his father's experience. He was wasting precious years if he didn't.

Someday the boy would realize his father's accomplishments were nothing to sneeze at. Tom Spader had scouted out the infrared footprints beneath the earth's surface and was now able to cross at will into the parallel universe and ever closer to the source. He must make the boy comprehend the momentousness of this act: a black man, taking a midnight stroll through a residential neighborhood in Greenwich, even carrying a jug of gasoline, for God's sake, and no sirens anywhere in the distance. Hello, Vagabond, he said to the Blaine dog, out tipping garbage cans. Vagabond, who'd been nursing a growl deep in his belly, whimpered hello.

The Crisps' most crucial shortcoming was that they were incapable of understanding that this was not a game of marbles. A good old-fashioned barbecue for two hundred negroes in one of the wealthiest suburbs in America is no longer simply a barbecue. A steak transforms into a genuine stake, as does the pile of watermelons left, defiantly, in plain view on the lawn. Gospel spirituals emanating from speakers placed on outdoor tables become knives, dull yet bared.

He'd been watching the Crisps since the day they moved in and had deduced they were not fools. They were well aware of the surveillance teams. The curious looks on the children's faces as they rolled watermelons to the periphery of the neighbor's yard but not one foot farther informed him that the Crisp relatives had been warned, as had his own son, of eyes watching them from behind brocade curtains. Yet the Crisps, unfortunately, did not comprehend the unshakable complexities of living watched lives. They believed, simplistically, that Greenwich air infused with the smell of their own barbecue could be a victory in itself; they believed that twelve horny black nephews could be the punchline of a joke told to a caucasian mailman, if one had enough cash in the bank. They were wrong.

According to Joe Klein, the mobilization had already begun. Realtors had been contracted, attics were being perused for valuable relics to take along. New Canaan, Joe had said with utmost casualness: "Meg and I took a drive through New Canaan last Sunday." New Canaan was higher, more secure ground: lily-white, ancient money. New Canaan would be difficult to penetrate, and then to negotiate, another odyssey for Tom to conquer from square one. Meanwhile, the black upper crust would tiptoe into Greenwich and onto Serendipity Street with their "antique" sofas, bought at discount furniture houses. Tom would begin to become associated in the minds of those who mattered with the impotent throng best known for wearing kente-cloth cummerbunds to ABA banquets. The bomb was ticking. Tom had just this one night to defuse it.

He twisted the cap loose on his jug of gasoline. This—he splashed a bit of liquid on the back door of the old Bonner house—was for dear Mabel and this—he trailed a bit of liquid as he walked along the dark porch in his dark shirt and dark pants—was for each of his children. That—he tossed twisted, soaked handkerchiefs, purchased just yesterday from a CVS twenty miles from home, onto the roof—that was for the little wilding niggers with the Mercedes pendants hanging from their necks who were going to grow to middle age in prison at a bang of his mallet later this week. The last was for the Crisps themselves, with the hope that their subsequent moves would be wiser. Tom sloshed his last bit of gasoline onto the gate of the white picket fence around the old Bonner house and stood there for a moment watching it drip long gray strings.

He lit a match. He watched the pillars begin to smoke.

There were many successful avenues of defense for a man accused of burning down property invaded by no-count negroes. Self-defense, for example, that always managed to work. And then there was Ignorance. Utter ignorance of the situation was the top-drawer, presidential defense, and he too had reached a high enough level to use it, if it came to that. Of course he knew nothing. He'd awoken to find a neighbor's house burnt to the ground, Norm Bonner's old place. Shocked the hell out of him. In fact, it's a goddamned eyesore, he'd say. Who's in charge of getting this pile of burnt rubble out of my view, he'd say. And if he inadvertently left some fingerprint tonight, he had reached that plateau where a fingerprint meant as little as the bruises on Anne Marie Bonner's jaw had meant the day her kidney finally failed.

The lock to a certain room began to crumble inside Tom's mind as he watched the Bonners' picture window mangle beneath the heat of the fire. It took several minutes before he realized something had gone terribly wrong: a certain door stood wide open in his mind, held open by a gale-force wind. He forced himself to break his gaze, to concentrate on shutting the door. His eyes shot back to the fire of their own accord, watched it dance slow mambos up the drain pipes on either side of the face of the house. It was hypnotic, the fire. Burned yellow. Burned yellow as a white woman's hair.

Ask someone in the Mississippi Delta who Emmett Till was, best have time on your hands for a story. Get close enough to

Leflore County, the storyteller could be colored or white, but one part of the story would always mesh: that Emmett Till business rocked the boat in Mississippi.

Tom could see that boy, strutting in his white buck shoes and his pants and his hat in front of Roy Bryant's Grocery. Yes, they'd had fun that day, listening to Emmett crow about Chicago, promising to take them to jazz clubs, because they were all going to make it to Chicago in a few years. Why, they'd never seen a colored boy strut that way . . . Cocky as the devil. And then they'd seen Roy Bryant stroll behind Emmett like a wolf, and they'd all quit laughing.

Boy's face when they found him was something to see, looked like a basket of muffins. Beaten, drowned, shot, everything. Boy's mama in Chicago stirred things up with all that talk about justice. Talked to northern newspapers, had *Jet* print photographs, got the eyes of folk all over the world trained on Leflore for that one hot minute. Then they all pulled out, packed up the cameras, left local niggers to hot-step across a bed of coals lit by outsiders. Mamma wouldn't speak the name Emmett Till, not even if the door was bolted. Emmett got his the summer of fifty-five. Tom got his that next winter.

White fellow named Avery Carter had been heard speaking Tom Spader's name in public. Nigger thought he was smart. Nigger's mama kept him out of the fields the full four months of winter and sent him to school. Drafty cabin what that nigger lived in held a shelf full of books, each one thicker than a white man's thigh. Nigger's mama told that redbone boy he was gonna end up something special, told him that even with decent white folk in the vicinity having to hear that filth. Colored folk spent all winter warning Tom's mamma. He ain't no little boy no more, best teach him to stick some gumption behind his Yassuh, Mr. Chancey, Suh. Mamma'd snap right back that her boy wasn't 'bout all that yassuh business. Don't come around preaching at her how to raise her child, she'd tell them. Folk would leave the shack muttering how Ethel Spader must believe misery couldn't speak her name just because she laid up there with Mr. Charlie, doing his so-called extra chores around the house. Ought to realize it was all a them strung together in this soup side by side. That boy don't learn to say Yassuh a little louder, no telling whose boy would end up paying for it. Ain't gonna be my boy, I'll see to that, they'd warn. Mamma'd let the doorknob hit 'em where the good Lord split 'em, and then wedge a chair beneath it to bolt it shut.

White folk began to step out of their shacks whenever Tom Spader passed by, grinning as if they'd found meat in a tooth. By February, white and colored alike were predicting Tom Spader's lynching the same way they predicted a change in the weather. Some folks had money on it: dead by April. Old colored women who used to call out Hey, Good-Lookin' when he strutted by with his schoolbooks all done up in a strap turned their cheeks toward the sun that winter.

Mamma stopped reading her Bible at night and began paying close attention to the cobwebs in the ceiling corners. The only conversation she'd make was about spiders laying eggs in her walls, hard as she worked to keep that place clean. Trees Tom had scaled as a boy scratched like claws against the cabin walls and windows.

Tom carried his terror in his chest, a pulsing lump of lard. By the night Avery Carter finally came knocking, Tom's neck was already raw from his own rubbing and scratching. Mamma rocked furiously in her chair that night while they yanked him outdoors, her eyes gone blind.

Nigger raped my sister, Avery Carter pronounced when he and the fellows prodding Tom along with sticks reached the designated clearing, voice hoarse and slurred from Wild Turkey. Another fellow bound Tom's legs with a ripped shirt and stepped back to admire his handiwork. War whoops filled the air and thick pale arms began to fling rocks through the dark. One struck Tom's temple and opened a gush of blood, and Avery Carter himself became Tom's unlikely savior, deflecting the rain of rocks with his meaty shoulder.

"It's my nigger," shouted Avery. "I'm running this show!"

"Ain't got all night!" shouted somebody back.

"Shut that damn trap," said Avery Carter. "Else I'll shut it for you!"

Tom pressed his eyes shut and waited for the noose to be fitted around his neck, but Avery paced in circles, swigging his Wild Turkey, enchanted by his own voice. He could have been reciting *Hamlet* rather than providing the self-appointed jurors with a graphic description of the brutal raping of his yellow-haired sister Sally, whom everybody in Leflore County knew was fat with a baby that would eventually, long after Tom's execution, come squawking out bearing an extremely strong Carter family resemblance, far stronger than even Mississippi state law allowed.

"Hand me the rope," said Avery finally, shoving his flask deep into his back pocket and cracking his knuckles.

"I know you ain't lookin' at me!" hooted Earl Rutherford, equally drunk.

"You brung the rope, din't ya?"

"What rope? Ain't nobody said nothin' about me bringin' no rope."

"You ain't got the rope?"

"Naw I ain't got it!"

"Then who brung it? I said, who brung the goddamn rope?"

"You probably forgot it on purpose so we couldn't hang him, you nigger lover you!"

During the months that Tom had tried to prepare himself mentally for his hanging, a strange idea had begun to lick at him. It wasn't the sort of idea he could give voice to. He hadn't even told Mamma, as she batted at her cobwebs with the broom, of the strange new worlds taking shape in his mind.

It all started when Miss Charlotte, Tom's math teacher that winter, had come by one night to leave twelve dollars for a train ticket and an offer to board at her brother's house up in Lovejoy, Illinois, both of which Mamma refused. Miss Charlotte had tried to explain it to Mamma, that the boy must run, that each nightfall was a golden opportunity. Be realistic,

Miss Charlotte told Mamma, both women bawling, but all Mamma would say was No, not my child.

Then there was old Preacher Huss, who'd sat with them and talked all night about Jesus being the bus driver to the Holy Land. About every colored person getting a front-row ticket on that bus, yes, indeedy. Every one of us colored gone be right up there in the front row watching those pearly gates open before our very eyes, he'd promised Tom, who'd only scratched crazily at his neck in response.

About the time the first green springtime buds began to sprout, Tom had begun to think about the fellows he knew who'd been lynched. There was Sweet Willie Bund, whipped two crackers despite their rifles and lived to tell about it for twenty-four hours. Lived that extra day only because Harley Hooper's wife went into labor and forbade him to kill a nigger on the day of his child's birth in case God had his eye pinned on the Hooper house. Don't whup the dawg today neither, Mrs. Hooper had yelled after him, according to beautiful Georgia Johnson, who nursed their elder children.

And Two-Shoe Smith. Boy's own mama had warned Two-Shoe to quit saying Nat and Turner in the same breath unless he felt like getting his testicles sheared off. They hog-tied that boy. Bound him up with masking tape and let him flap like a fish on the bed of Pete Helm's pickup truck as they paraded him through town. Left him for dead, but Two-Shoe crawled all the way to Tallahatchie on elbows and knees, organs gripped in his fist.

Then there was Emmett Till, killed for stretching a toe over a line that could not logically exist. Tom Spader, his bound feet sinking into the mud beneath the stars as he waited to die, remembered Emmett, strutting, tipping his hat, popping a wad of bubblegum loud as he pleased. And suddenly, all the ideas that had been struggling to coalesce in his terrorized mind all these months merged and blossomed. As clearly as he saw Avery and Earl tearing the shirts off their backs to brawl in the moonlight, he saw truth laid bare.

An alternate universe existed. An intergalactic mix-up had occurred at some point, the wrong key had been turned, reality had been mangled. Somewhere, there was another land, remarkably similar to this one atmospherically, where colored boys could strut if they chose without risking murder. A series of slivers of reality, or time, or space, on—he would call it Gamma—had been interchanged with precisely pro-portionate slivers of reality from Earth. Colored folk being forever on the bottom of the barrel was actually, he suddenly realized as he fought to maintain his footing in the marsh, quite a good deal more complicated than a crying shame. At the very same instant that the hangman's noose was finally located belting the youngest Carter brother's pants, Tom Spader began to realize that he was the savior, the messiah. He was the man burdened by God with the task of finding the key and leading his people home.

Under the night sky, his executioners managed to find something further to brawl about, as if they had all the time in the world to commit this murder, which in fact they did. Meanwhile, Tom Spader reflected upon why he had been marked for this lynching. Somebody, although Tom doubted it could be somebody as ignorant as Avery Carter, understood that Tom Spader had spotted the seam in the fabric. Somebody—and Tom envisioned a tribunal of white men in dark suits—realized that this young boy had managed to see beyond the web of dead ends. Tom Spader was, in effect, not principally being killed. More accurately, his death was a preventative measure, analogous to Mamma chewing on raw garlic to ward off sickness.

Out of the darkness, Avery Carter lunged at Tom, who still stood immobilized within his binding. Earl flew simultaneously through the air and caught Avery with a solitary finger through a dungaree belt loop, snatching him back. The men once again sank into the mud, pummeling each other. As Avery's legs slurped through puddles, Tom knew definitively that none of these morons charged with overseeing his execution would have been entrusted with the secrets he needed to root out. Tom's life's purpose, he realized at that instant, was to somehow locate the keepers of the Gammanian key, and to realign the universe.

Tom saw it not as a miracle but rather as a vote of confidence from some neutral panel of judges high above the Milky Way that his executioners were so engrossed in their noisy, drunken fight that he was able to fall backward into the swamp without the splash being detected by anybody except the youngest Carter brother, whose eyes growing round as Coke bottlecaps were the last sight Tom saw before he sank, arms and legs still bound, into the murky waters.

He floated like a corpse, remaining in and around the swamp for almost a week as the dogs barked and men chopped through the thicket with machetes. The sharecropper who rescued him informed him that his dear mother was already dead, a pair of borrowed scissors plunged through her heart the very same night her boy was snatched away. The man pressed on him a balled-up handkerchief that contained enough colored folk's money to buy a ticket out of town. People round here, myself included in with the rest of 'em, he told Tom with moist eyes, be just as glad to see you gone, all this trouble ya'll done stirred up.

He'd taken the train to Lovejoy and arrived to find ... more idiots! Negroes, watching him suspiciously. Colored folk satisfied with their mangled reality. First thing he'd done when he got off that train to Lovejoy was to punch one of those little niggers standing in line to see Tyrone Power save the day. Stupid sonofabitch little nigger, stupid coon to come dancing out at him, pounding his fists into his chest. Fool. Idiot, stupid brainless idiot, there wasn't time to be suspicious of one another. He should have smashed his skull.

But then—Mabel's smile. Dark chocolate lips smiling out from a sea of mistrust. Sweet Mabel. He was drawn to her, almost as if she'd beckoned him to her. She'd understood not to ask questions, to put her trust in him. Mabel. The only person on earth who understood he was irretractably enmeshed in a lifelong mission. Dear sweet Mabel.

Mabel. Tom staggered out of his reverie. He was covered with sweat, and there were sirens in the distance, coming closer each second. His mamma's face lanced out at him and he grabbed his own head, fought with it. He'd never gone back. How could he, Mamma lying in a pauper's grave, Mamma and those rusty scissors. Emmett, head full of muffins. The chair, tied to the door at night, watching its legs jiggle when a truck sped past. The fire, just watch the fire burn, just concentrate on the fire, it was so much easier that way.

A fire engine turned onto Serendipity Street, its siren turned low and almost soothing. Lights began to come on in houses. He forced his legs to move slowly. Do not run— cardinal rule!—never run until you have no other choice. Whoo hoo, white boys whooping. Mamma's eyes, willfully gone blind.

"Judge Spader? Is that you there? How about this fire?"

Hold arm up, wave, say something. Say something, for Christ's sake. Say Something *Or It's All Over.* Our father, who art in heaven. Something, anything.

"Why hello there, Clyde. We're lit up like the Fourth of July tonight." All right then, good, hope there's no soot on my face. Shake head in amazement. Mamma plunging scissors into her chest in a dreary, empty room. Got to stamp her out, got to close the door. "Glad we've got you fellows."

"Glad to be of service. You mind stepping back to the curb, Judge Spader? Wouldn't want you to get hurt."

Walk slowly, wave, a hello. "Don't mind at all." Move toward the group of gathering neighbors, direct them back, tell them to get back to the curb, so nobody gets hurt. Tell them their homes are safe. Tell them everything is going to be all right. Stay calm. Stay with them. Stay close as white on rice.

Man ought to learn his job, in Mabel's opinion. If that scrawny fire captain knew his job, this investigation would have been wrapped up days ago. He wouldn't have had to bring the fire marshal out here to nose around. Acting like some big shot out there in his plastic helmet, probably getting a kick out of making folk think something was wrong, thinking he was upset, thinking he'd found some little inconsequential piece of evidence that probably didn't mean a damn thing. Mabel didn't need all this excitement today. She had a husband upstairs sick in bed. Very sick. Double pneumonia, she'd told Cissy over at his office. Although it might be some kind of virus.

She walked back to the window. That houseburning was local kids running some kind of initiation, that's what the firefighters had said that night, and they ought to know, who would know better than the men right there at the scene fighting the fire. Mabel could see how this city operated, just trying to stir something up to justify the city budget. Supposed to be a high-class suburb, acting this way. Man ought to go home to his wife. Nobody got hurt in that fire. Go on home, she said to the windowpane. Leave folk in peace.

Back again to the window. She sniffed, wiped her eyes, crying from that awful odor, worse than onions. She didn't have time for this. Royetta had up and quit yesterday, just when this house needed its spring cleaning. One eye out the window, Mabel loaded the sofa cushions in a pile. She'd beat them. Get that stench out of this house. Had their police tape wrapped around all the pine trees as if some serious crime had been committed, when everyone knew it was only a prank gone haywire. The nerve of those people. Only half realizing what she was doing, Mabel reached for the phone and dialed a number and just as suddenly replaced it in the cradle. Ma was dead.

She paced back to the window. There never were people milling around on Serendipity, it wasn't that kind of neighborhood. But today it seemed as lonely as a ghost town after a shootout. Not a soul out there but that fire marshal and his men, deciding everybody's fate. Just kicking up dust, just putting on a show. Mabel stood in the center of her living room and wrung her hands.

This smell was about to drive Mabel insane, she felt as though she was walking toward a cliff every time she paced past the picture window. She ought to wash these walls. Smells tucked themselves into walls and hid. Mabel sat down on the sofa, falling farther than she'd expected because she'd forgotten the cushions were off. She tried to focus. Whatever this was smelling up her house, Lord, but she wished she could figure out how to flood it out of here without any of the neighbors noticing. They'd notice thrown-open windows and curtains, nobody on this street aired their house out that way but Ruth Crisp. Mabel could carry the cushions out back one by one, casually past the picture window, and beat them, or even right here where she stood, hardly moving. Mabel took a cushion off the pile and held it low, watching out the window as she beat it with a slow, hard fist.

From across the room she peered out the window and saw the captain running over to the fire marshal. She watched that white man trotting down her street and her heart went right in her throat. Two of them, heads stuck together now, the captain's mouth moving a mile a minute. Mabel wished she wore glasses, she could almost read the lips. She eyed the telephone. Everybody she could have called was dead. Had to be kids, the captain had said it just like that the night of the fire, and he'd sounded so positive she wished she had a tape of it. He'd said it was kids, and nobody else had said anything else or thought anything else. No, he was not . . . he couldn't be . . . he was pointing out houses. He was pointing out the Spader house. Mabel dropped to her knees and somehow ended up with the phone in her hand again.

———

"Baby, wake up. Baby, it's for you."

"Huh? Hello?"

"And tell homegirl she better learn how to speak to LaKisha. And to don't be waking nobody man up at no seven A.M., else I might have to kick some ass."

"Tommy? Tommytwo, are you there? It's your mother."

Oh man. It was Mom. He shook the sleep out of his brain. "Hi, Mom. You're up early."

"I know it's early, son, but I have something to tell you. Son? Is there somebody in your room with you?"

"Yeah, Mom. We're studying for finals."

"Oh Tommy, oh son, oh baby. I'm so sorry. It's my fault, it's my fault."

"Mom, what's wrong?"

"Oh Tommy. It's your father." Mom sucked in her breath.

His mom was crying. It was awful. Fuck, Dad was dead. Dad was dead. Fuck.

"Oh gawwwd, Mom!"

"Tommy? Son? Can you hear me? Morehouse never should have been an issue with your father. He should have been bursting with pride to have a son at Morehouse. Tommy, can you hear me?"

"What? Oh God, Mom, that doesn't even matter any-more . . ."

"Let me finish. I never should have whipped you over that whole issue. Now your sisters deserved what they got, they should have been pleased they hadn't had to go out and work for that Pinto, but you on the other hand hadn't done a thing but wanted to go to school with some other black children—"

"Mom, stop crying, I can't understand—"

"Hear me, Tommytwo. Parents do their best by their chil-dren. There are no ground rules in that situation."

"Mom, what are you talking about? Mom, look, is Dad dead?"

"Dead? Your father? No, no. No. It's only the flu. Don't you worry." Mabel blew her nose. "Mama's got it under control."

Tommytwo tried to get it straight, but LaKisha was expos-ing her big belly at him. Dad must be threatening not to pay

next year's fees again. Mom must be going through menopause. Fucking weird family.

LaKisha lifted her maternity nightgown over her head. Her
breasts and belly seemed one more spoonful bigger this
morning than they had last night. That was his kid in there,
just about ready to come bursting out, and that was his ring
on her finger. LaKisha grasped him tight and they rolled
around together naked on the bed and he felt his baby kick
and LaKisha kissed his eyelids. A great studio apartment,
summer session's tuition on his woman's ring finger, a job
lined up at Atlanta's best video store and where one of
his boys was manager, a baby on the way. Yes, Dad: Nigger
Heaven, and loving every minute.

"Mom? I gotta go study for my final."

"All right, baby boy. Mama loves you."

"Who can spell 'discover,' " said Hilary, starting class, even
angrier than usual. Teacher's break? Teacher's break nothing.
She hated that teachers' lounge. She wouldn't be surprised if
she ended up killing somebody someday in there. Carlotta almost got hers today, in there championing the curriculum
guide. Yes, Carlotta, Columbus Discovered the Indians, but
guess what, The Indians Discovered Him Too! Why was it always such hard work for white people to grasp the simple
fact that others besides themselves had relevant points of
view . . . Oh Christ, Hilary, just shut up, it's over, concentrate
on teaching class. Hilary jabbed a finger toward Jesus, the

only Puerto Rican kid in third grade, who got a beating each and every night for having to take summer school with a bunch of retarded niggers. Hilary felt like kicking some ass herself.

"Discuvah," said Jesus, playing. *"P-e-f."*

"Boy, sit down."

The machinery had clicked into place, no need anymore to hunt niggers down and chop off their balls and rape the maid. Just keep electing benignly neglectful presidents and implanting Brave White Men stories in all the citizens' minds from an early age. That was what she ought to be teaching these children: how this country really worked.

"FaShawn, spell 'discover.' "

Just say discover, that bitch Carlotta had sat on that old vinyl sofa filing her fingernails, eyes downcast as if she was tired of this whole damn discussion. Just say Columbus discovered America—and then, low and disgusted—for Christ's sake, Hilary, give it a rest, they're just third graders. Not even financially stable, that Carlotta, had a mother living in a trailer home, but might as well be a pit bull, out there protecting their precious status quo.

" 'Discover'," said FaShawn. "Start with a *B*."

"*D*, remember? It starts with a *D*."

And yes, Carlotta, I know you didn't start slavery, but what motherfucker did? No reason in the goddamn world people of color had to be the only ones out there trying to figure it all out while They lie back on their fat asses proclaiming racism is over, as if a couple of civil rights acts could wipe out a virus. Evil, pure evil. She took a deep breath, trying to clear her mind of enough hate to concentrate on teaching class.

" 'Discover'," said Hilary, rapping the desk with her knuckles to revive the sleepers. "Who's next?" Bonjour's mouth formed the shape of a *U* and Hilary braced herself. Idiots. These kids were idiots. Not a child in the room could spell "cat." An utter embarrassment. Practically every third grader with pigment in the entire district was enrolled in summer school, trying to make up the classes they'd already flunked at eight years old. And each day she had to reteach all twenty-six letters just to get them to spell the word of the day. A vast blue-green horizon dotted with red brick fortresses suddenly flooded Hilary's mind.

Oh. They were blocked. Their spelling function was locked away behind thick walls.

Hilary stopped, stunned. What was going on? It felt like some sort of . . . revelation. Here it came again: Bam! She'd made another grave mistake! She'd been wrong about white people, all these years! Hilary had to catch her balance against the desk. White people weren't demons. Repeat: not demons. They were . . . stupid . . . blocked. Didn't have the ability to perceive the complexities . . . missing the faculties of comprehension . . . blind to the infinite permutations of their very own race game . . . another repercussion of slavery . . .

The children giggled and squealed and Tomasena hit Jacquita and Marcus and Jonathan got in a shoving match as Hilary stood beside her desk, rocking ever so slightly, chalk in her fist. The curriculum guide's insistence that Columbus Discovered America, this whole walk in a straight line to the lunchroom, even this insane national mantra about color-blindness and bootstraps was . . . nothing but desperate camouflage . . . masking a . . . a mass psychological malfunction. Charleyanna was displaying her underpants to the rest of the class and Donny was cootie-fying his desk by rubbing saliva into the wood. Columbus Discovered America, Hilary whispered to herself, hands shaking like her mother's, trying to jolt herself back to earth.

Oh God, no. They were shimmying. They hadn't even been there a moment ago, and now they were shimmying like diamonds, filling in what used to be invisible air. Fire, Hilary barked through her mind—typical white-man tactics! Burned down that house to keep a black woman from buying it and every last cracker on Serendipity Street probably knew exactly who did it, probably chipped in money for a medal! No wonder Mabel had sounded so hysterical on the phone!

No, it was useless. Hilary couldn't rile herself back up. There was no anger left. It was gone. Just like that, just that easy. She'd been set free. The smell of the children intensified as if each was a flower. The room was glowing. The Creator was so clearly here, with her, and so blessedly clearly not a white man with a beard, but streams of pure energy, plentiful, beautiful, bountiful energy. She saw an image of Carlotta, and she saw walls within Carlotta's mind, and she saw the lightbulbs out in certain compartments. A tidal wave of compassion nearly swept her off her feet. Stormy, that white-acting heifer! Nothing. No hate left.

"Why Miss Spader smiling?"

"Miss Spader, it be game time?"

No, it couldn't be game time, they had to get through the textbook section on Columbus, and then they had two-digit subtraction. Didn't they?

But then again, why? Fools had led long enough! *"D-i-s-c-o-v-e-r,"* spelled Hilary, because measuring a child's worth by spelling prowess was pure insanity, and the kids said Ooo! Ooo! and some ran back to get their notebooks. (. . . begin to nurture more fundamental forms of intelligence . . .). Hilary cocked an ear, listening, waiting. Children's hands were encircling her waist and wrists, and the little legs were skipping beside her toward the windowseat in the corner, which Hilary suddenly understood was the only place in the classroom fit for humanity. She let the children tug her to the cushion and felt small strong arms wind around her neck the moment she sat.

She purred with pleasure when the voice returned, enveloping her, murmuring something delicious about knowledge, telling her to let the top spin, let all the worms out of the can, end the entire concept of taboos, hear these children's truths, name it knowledge, add it to the human bank of knowledge. "Why don't our textbooks say the Indians 'discovered' Columbus?" Hilary called out giddily, winding her legs beneath her in the windowseat. She praised God (praised God? Yes, praised God!) for letting her witness magic: the confusion, the disbelief, the giggling behind small brown fists. And the children, none of whom could spell "cat," began picking their noses and jumping off the windowsill and taking the first small stabs at analyzing the world.

"Principal spoke ugly to my mama that time I got in the

fight out there where they got that tree at around where that—that—that—" said Juanita, nearly shrieking from the excitement. "He might could hate black people and that might could make him choosed those textbooks!"

"And Puerto Ricans, too," said Jesus, shoving girls' legs aside to try to lean in next to Hilary. The girls kicked him and Hilary felt fingers braiding through her hair and soft voices whispering, She got pretty hair. Miss Spader, you got some pretty hair. Entire fortresses within people's minds—the Creator was so original, so wildly creative, designing details so very twisted and meaningful! Another revelation, this time like a bolt of white light: WE ARE ALL THE CREATOR!!!

"But why he be like that if he 'POSED to be the principal," said Jaliqua, around a jawbreaker, "and we 'POSED to be living in a demotrussy?" Let the children's perspectives shimmer, yes, let this be her mission, for they were each holy. Charleyanna stuck her thumb in her mouth and stared at Hilary questioningly. Hilary rubbed her eyes. The children were actually shimmering. Oh God, not still more.

Noise . . . it was . . . incredible . . . the children's shouts but so much more, so loud, how could it be so loud, like a gospel symphony, or, somehow, a pot of thick soup. Donny clucked like a rooster while the other children debated, and the very whiteness of Donny's skin became part of the music. 'Cause they got to put in our head that they way is the right way, else things might could change, said Charleyanna, thumb popped out of her mouth for a moment, and the popping of the thumb was a drumbeat, and the eyelashes brushing the brown cheeks were a bright chord. Cops be shooting Puerto Ricans in the back of the head too, Jesus shouted in Mershawn's face. And Hilary's thoughts were suddenly no longer coalescing into their usual words and pictures. A bubble formed in her stomach and gurgled to the top of her throat. She tried to burp. That wasn't the problem.

Skiddleebiddleebeedumbaddaballachidickamuveeda, Hilary said, and clapped her mouth closed. That voice, it hadn't been hers. She felt her tongue fidgeting inside her mouth. Strange sounds—but somehow not strange at all—were forming themselves. Chiddleebedeebachagavaskiddleebad, Hilary whispered, stopping to gasp for breath every few seconds, and the girls played in her hair and one dropped her neck against Hilary's to hear what she was saying, then kissed her cheek and went back to braiding. Hilary held her mouth slightly ajar, and did not dare to close it again. She realized she had a rather enraptured look on her face that could get her instantly fired. But it didn't matter. Who cared, who cared, who cared if they fired her, who cared, who cared, who cared! Not I, Hilary rejoiced, and her lips sang prayers for all humanity.

"Aw, she just speaking in tongue. My granny be doing that," said Mershawn, stopping to listen, and then running back to the middle of the room, where the kids were doing somersaults.

The opening beats of "Push It" pumped out of speakers and shook the club floor like tremors. Stormy recognized it as a special request from Ramon, her boss. It was his way of telling her to get out of the bathroom and back up in the cage and dance. Yeah, yeah.

Stormy sang along with Salt-n-Pepa as she climbed into her cage. Tears came to her eyes. She pulled at her white miniskirt to make it tighter, more tantalizing. Not for the spectators below, but for her uterine lining. She was two days late, two long, hellish days. And in a Catholic country where you needed a—*hijo de puta!*—psychological evaluation to frigging abort. This white miniskirt was her last hope. At the deciding moment when a girl's uterine lining was doing its final eeny-meeny-miney-mo about whether to self-destruct or stay and feed the fetus, it took a peek at the outside world. If the first thing it glimpsed was a white miniskirt and white, newish underwear, out it came with a big whoosh, it couldn't resist. If this brand-new specially purchased snow-white miniskirt that she was ill able to afford didn't work, Stormy was taking the fast train to hanger city before this mother-fucker started growing fingers and toes.

Whoosh, she sang to the music, shimmying like never before, dipping way low. Whoosh, she begged her body, skidding her hips like they were riding a wave. Ramon—*cabron!*—had no idea how little five thousand pesetas plus tips meant to her on a night like tonight when what she needed was to be in her *pequeño apartamento* lighting certain candles and chanting promises at whoever's dead ancestors she might be able to conjure up. Ramon stuck stubby fingers in his mouth and whistled. Friday was the best night of the week for Ramon the Cabron. Friday was the night a girl could make a name for herself if she lit up the cage. A thousand faces were screaming out Eh-storm-ay! from the dance floor. After all these months working here, Ramon finally scraped the spotlight off big blond Yessica and onto Stormy. Unfortunately, tonight was one night she could give a damn whether all these spics and tourists wanted her body. She was dancing for herself tonight, dancing for her uterine lining. Just one spot, and she was blowing this popsicle stand for Saint-Tropez as a reward.

She felt a gush. Not a whoosh, just a gush. Maybe not even a gush, maybe just some sort of weird air pocket. But maybe a gush, maybe even a semi-whoosh. Wetness, anyway. She felt wetness when the wind hit, she was almost positive. Center stage, Stormy danced as hard as she could, twirling, snaking, soaring, praying.

———

Here she came. That Crisp woman, squat and square as a dump truck, storming up Serendipity Street. And here was Mabel—dammit—between maids just when she could have used somebody to open the door and lie. Thunder clapped in the distance, a storm was coming, and Mabel felt the exact same way. Last person on earth she felt like dealing with today was Ruth Crisp, and that was no lie.

Mabel peeked around the edge of the curtain. She'd figured it was just a matter of time before Ruth Crisp came barging over hurling accusations. Of course she was mad they'd burned down the house she'd wanted so bad. Mabel'd be mad too. But Ruth Crisp ought to just shut up and be glad she hadn't yet forked over any money. No need to come barging over here stirring everything back up now that the rubble was gone and the investigation was closed and Tom's jaw was back ticking. That was exactly what they wanted, an ashy, overweight lottery queen making wild accusations against Connecticut's first black state supreme court judge. She could hear them popping their little knuckles, rubbing their moist little palms together. She took a deep whiff of the curtain she was pinching between her fingers: Fine. Smelled like the dry cleaners, nothing but the dry cleaners.

Woman could have been shot out of a cannon, the way she was pounding up the Spader front walk, each step a true collision. Mabel cracked her neck from side to side and wound her arms in the air the same way they warmed up in yoga. She stepped into her two-hundred-dollar—four twenty-five before markdown—soft-as-butter Manolo Blahnik pumps, which she kept in the entryway closet, just for occasions like this when somebody tried to catch her off guard. Not every colored woman in America wore house slippers all day, and that was number one on the list of lessons Ruth Crisp needed to learn. Whatever that woman was clomping up Mabel's front walk to say, she wouldn't be the only one who'd get a chance to speak her piece today, no, ma'am. Mabel had a few choice nuggets on her own mind. She slapped a hand down the back of her neck: smooth as velvet. She snatched the door open wide.

"Why, hello," said Mabel. She tried to smile but it fell right off her face. No need to shovel it back on, any fool knew this was an awkward situation.

Ruth Crisp stood on Mabel's welcome mat, huffing and puffing and glaring and scratching. Not two teeth touching in the entire mouth and she had the nerve to be coming over here trying to start trouble with decent people who'd done exactly what people were put on this planet to do: raised three fine children in a decent home. And meanwhile, whoever that little brownskin girl was Mabel'd seen driving around here lately in that flashy red Maserati, either that was a bowling ball stuck up under her dress or else she was six months pregnant. Woman had some nerve, storming up here as if she—she of all people!—had papers on Mabel.

Suddenly, Ruth Crisp twisted her neck around and started scratching so hard all Mabel could think was psoriasis. Aunt Hattie used to have psoriasis, used to cut a potato to rub on it every night. Ruth Crisp scratched in silence for what seemed like more than a minute. Scratched so hard a bobby pin finally surrendered and dropped to the stoop with a clink. Lo and behold, a good four inches of hair came tumbling down to Ruth Crisp's shoulders. Fell in a clump. Mabel leaned back and blinked. She'd had no idea that woman had all that hair. And bouncy too, fell right down when the pin dropped out.

"Is the judge home?" said Ruth Crisp.

No way to explain it, but seeing Ruth Crisp's hair made Mabel come all discombobulated. Now, how in the world had that woman managed to grow all that hair, bad a grade as she had, Mabel would like to know. It wasn't a wig, Mabel had seen enough wigs in her day to know a wig. Couldn't be a wig. It wasn't till thunder clapped again and Mabel nearly fell over that she realized just how far off her guard she'd fallen, looking at that thick head of hair. She'd never seen the woman this close up before, but she would have sworn Ruth Crisp couldn't have more than a teaspoon of fuzz up there. Holding out pretty well against all this humidity too.

"Judge home?" said Ruth Crisp, loud.

"My husband? Why, no."

As a matter of fact, Mabel'd swear on the Bible there'd been times when she'd seen that woman's scalp gleaming through all the way from up the street. Head normally looked like a cat toy, especially around the back edges. Standing there in her own doorway, Mabel felt almost frightened. Lord, ever since the fire, she'd sensed Judgment Day was coming, things were finally spiraling out of control. Ruth Crisp clawed at her neck once again.

"Damn weave," muttered Ruth Crisp. "Dropped five hundred dollars down a garbage disposal trying to look like Diana Ross."

A weave, thought Mabel, fanning her bosom. So that was what this miracle boiled down to. At least she was making some effort to seem less like a banshee. Ruth Crisp doubled over, pulling sections apart to scratch deeper. Mabel couldn't help but lean in, take a look for herself.

She squinted into Ruth Crisp's scalp and saw the hair so short and nappy it could have been stitches, with strands cut out of somebody else's head pasted directly onto the skin itself. The scent of Ultra Sheen passed up Mabel's nose, blue and creamy. Odd thing was, Mabel sniffed at that woman's head on purpose. Felt like a kind of truth serum, coursing through her body.

Yes, Mabel'd smelled the gasoline everywhere she turned while he ate his breakfast that next day—on the walls, the curtains, the sofa cushions. Nobody else had a nose like Mabel's, she'd smelled it all. She'd tracked that gasoline to his hands, picked it up under black coffee, turkey bacon, and scrambled eggs with blue cheese, as well as at least two showers with Lava Soap, which Mabel knew was one brand she never kept in the house. That Lava Soap must have been bought special, not to mention the gasoline.

"You busy?" said Ruth Crisp, stepping a foot inside Mabel's door. Mabel swallowed, dry as cotton candy, and moved aside to let the woman in.

"Go on kick your shoes off," sighed Mabel as Ruth Crisp slid and nearly broke her back on these damn hardwood floors Mabel had never liked in the first place. She toed out of her own Manolo Blahniks. No need to be the only one clomping around the house on these knitting needle heels, that was for damn sure. And don't tell Mabel to turn her husband in to some white cop for the sake of blind justice. This very morning Mabel forgot to wear her birthday ruby to the cheese shop, and came out of there blood boiling. Boiling! Boiled like a pot of oil, snatched her breath away, took three years off her life. Let them write a law to prevent that, muttered Mabel, leading Ruth Crisp down the hallway, before we sit here talking about blind justice. Then and only then.

And she didn't need to hear about any psychiatrists either. He simply bought gasoline and simply burned that house down, Mabel could say, and she could call the insane asylum. But they'd have to cart her away with him, because as quiet a life as she led, Lord knew she had contemplated worse than arson. She pinched two fingers together, waved them in the air as she led Ruth Crisp back to the kitchen. That was exactly how close the cheese shop cashier had come to getting her head chopped off with her own cheese knife this very morning. Was the Gruyère a hit, Odetta, Mabel's black behind. Mabel could have burned down a dozen houses over the years.

Mabel took another whiff of Ruth Crisp's head as the woman sat, and her nose filled with Ultra Sheen and weave glue and edges singed with a hot iron and somehow it gave Mabel the strength to admit what was really down at the bottom of it all. Tom Spader was terrified. Tom Spader was a fist of terror, and he'd been one the day she'd agreed to marry him and he was always going to be one. Terror had looked like something better when it was buried inside of a handsome young man with green eyes who stood taller than her daddy. Terror had made that man seem as exciting as a shooting star—Mabel knew exactly why Becka and these other white women lost their minds over dark meat.

"Ma was terrified too," Mabel realized for the very first time. Woman paid her in rotten strawberries, and wasn't a thing Mama could say or do.

"My ma still back in Florida. Won't come up. Cain't say I blame her. Cain't say I blame her," Ruth Crisp said, answering what she thought was a question.

He'd had no fever this past week, no signs of flu or

pneumonia or anything classifiable. Just a stark gray terror, circling his eyes and splitting the skin at the corners of his mouth into tight white strips. His fists stayed white and dry from being clenched. When he slept, he grew quiet and still, and it was as though she were sleeping beside a corpse.

What broke Mabel's heart was to hear him calling out to his mama. This he did while wide awake, many more times than a grown man ought to ever have to, particularly while his wife was standing there wiping away drool. Help . . . Me, he'd say, wild-eyed, and then he'd moan and cry and plead for his mama. Then for long stretches, he went to work: he clenched his body, from legs to temples, with his eyes jammed shut, and she learned not to ask if he needed the bedpan. White folk, Mabel figured, although she didn't know for sure.

Each morning for six long days, she kept the curtains drawn and fed him soup like a baby bird. She lay there beside him watching all the little pregnant black girls they loved to show on daytime TV. If the babydaddy suddenly drop off a edge, the babymama need to be there for they baby, she learned how to say, and she would chant it like a mantra, praying that man would hang on and not lose his mind completely. Lord, not Tom.

By the third day, she was praying to the black God, Allah. This man has done so much for the race, she begged, I know you can see it. Allah, please don't take my man away from me, he made one mistake, and you can see how it's killing him. She happened to floss her teeth one night in bed, the way she'd probably start doing if Tom were dead, and cried for half an hour believing he really would die, realizing life as she knew it was over, in a thousand unwelcome ways.

So the man had burned down a house, she was yelling at Jesus Christ himself by day five. Big deal! Plenty of soldiers had killed plenty of other soldiers in plenty of wars. Whitey could fly to any third-world country and kill whomever, for whatever reason. And you let these little black and Hispanic kids ride through neighborhoods shooting at people on porches—kids who ought to be in school, finally learning something after all these centuries. No. Do not come up in Mabel's face preaching about morality now, not with the amount of hate you leave us down here festering in. You go save the porpoises, Mabel told Jesus. I'll judge my own man.

Then last night around midnight, she turned on *Johnny Carson*. Tom Jones, the singer, was making a comeback, which Mabel felt drawn to witness, for some odd reason. Good thing Tom was asleep, because Tom Jones was Tom Spader's least favorite type of white man. And in a melancholy mood, she slipped on a silver peignoir. She lay on her side of the bed and she listened to Tom Jones singing and she massaged a tired old sore: More visits to Lovejoy would have had those children confused, all those old people reminding them about all the brick walls they'd have to face in their lives, never giving the idea a chance that things could possibly be different for the next generation, that this world could very well turn out to be their oyster, which it had. Hilary certainly had sounded ecstatic when she'd called earlier from the ashcan? ashtray? ashram?—some kind of spa, Mabel supposed—where she was visiting. And Tommytwo was a mother's dream, busy studying for his finals. And that Stormy, she was soaking up all kinds of culture over there in Spain, according to her letters. All three children were doing better than she could have imagined.

And Ma had always gotten her envelope full of school pictures at the beginning of every single school year—out of the corner of Mabel's eye, bathed in the blue light of the television, she saw Tom Spader's sleeping body begin to clench beside her. Looked like he was bracing for a punch.

He flipped onto his stomach, still in a deep sleep, a boxer trying to stumble to his feet. He began to kick so violently that she could hear muffled springs squeaking within the bed. And he began to snore awfully, sawing logs, with a horrible cough imbedded in the middle of each snore somehow. Anger, rising up.

Mabel patted around and found the remote and pressed the volume button and made Tom Jones's singing louder, which made Tom's violence increase by the same amount. She hadn't seen that kind of fury on Tom's face since that first day he'd come to Lovejoy. The anger of a wild animal, thrashing and ravaging another little boy he had never even said hello to. She watched her husband sit bolt upright, then fall back against the mattress, and his temples began to throb as if an orchestra conductor were striking up a symphony inside. *Tick tock tick. Tick tock tock. Tick. Tock. Tick. Tock. Tick, tock, tick, tock.*

And Mabel began to cry. She cried like a baby and then she

began to laugh. She cried like a baby and laughed like a loon, and all she felt was love, nothing but the same aching love she felt for the children. Which shook her up a little bit, because she had never quite gotten to that level about Tom before.

She dropped down and buried her face in his chest, and he reached to kiss her head. She would have company for the next leg of her journey. She would not yet have to walk this world alone. Later on into the night, she'd found the MTV channel and she'd done her Sweet Potato, right there on the bed, with Tom admiring from his pillow. She would not have to walk this world alone.

A bowlegged, ashy-kneed crack addict on *Geraldo Rivera* got up out of her chair the other day to tell a skanky piece of poor white trash whose ménage à trois had gone awry: Work wit the homeboy you already got, because he seem like he worf it. And although such a streetish woman could not tell Mabel a thing, the words struck a chord within her. She loved Tom Spader, period. She was going to fix him up, try to bring him to a point where he had a little more love inside to work with.

Her first step was to piece it all together, like a puzzle, all of it, from the very beginning. This couldn't have been part of Tom's grand scheme—burning down a house! and the house a sister was trying to buy, at that. Except that Tom *was* now a confirmed supreme court black justice—first black supreme court judge, state supreme justice, court state judge, oh, Mabel never could quite get it right.

That boy had always had ambition. Set his mind on dreams

more magnificent than anyone she'd ever known, except of course for men like Pea Pie, who'd seemed to want to be crowned the African king. Who Mabel almost ended up marrying. Whose drivel Mabel could have ended up listening to all day long while she washed sheets. Mabel had a secret, and she'd never told it to anyone, and it probably had nothing to do with anything anyway . . . Extenuating circumstances Mabel's behind, it was her turn to decide what was relevant and what wasn't.

"I smelled Tom Spader before I ever saw him," Mabel said aloud in her kitchen. "Sniffed him right to me."

Ruth Crisp, in her nylon footies, was pushing aside Mabel's salt and pepper shakers and standing her handbag on the countertop. "Say what?"

Slow down, Mabel told herself. Don't be a fool. Yes, something about the aroma of the woman's hair oil helps you think straight, but don't start telling her all about your smelling powers and admitting Tom burned down the house she almost bought and laying yourself wide open. Not yet. Look at the bag. Louis Vuitton—all right, Mabel herself had once paid three hundred dollars for pleather just because she'd seen a white woman do it. But all that bought hair pasted on her scalp—Mabel did not know this woman. Before she started pouring out her business to a stranger she had never said more than boo to, she'd better see what sorts of legal papers were in that bag.

Ruth Crisp unzipped her bag. Took out a bottle. Another one, and another. All of them blue, but different sizes and shapes, one with a spray spout. Lined them up on the kitchen counter. Must have been fifteen bottles, and all of them had "Amway" scrawled across the front in fancy blue script.

Amway. How about that. Selling Amway. Mabel began to feel just the slightest bit giddy.

"Everybody know somebody selling Amway," pitched Ruth Crisp, sounding as disgusted as those colored cashiers they used to bus in to work at the downtown McDonald's. "But some of this garbage really do work . . ."

"What's this one do?" Mabel couldn't help but giggle. Woman was selling Amway. Thirteen million dollars, and selling Amway to the neighbors. Black folks' lives were always such an adventure.

"That one? That's for when you run out the bleach to clean the tub and toilet."

"Excuse me, but . . . aren't you a millionaire?"

"Shoot. I'm a hold onto that money *tight*. Plenty these colored folk get some money and still be dying broke. I know you seen that colored negro won the New Jersey lottery a few years back with the wife on one arm? and the girlfriend on the other? and the poke-pie hat? Spent it. Not me. Greenwich my home for good." Ruth Crisp stopped to take a breath, then revved right back up—

"That child of mine—I know you seen my play niece driving around in a Maserati—but that's a whole nother story, I might get to it later. I told her, Tampiqua! at least get you a Amway distributor's kit to pay the insurance and gas money, but Miss Tampiqua, she shy, she want Auntie to start her off finding customers—"

"Wait." This woman could talk an ear off. Mabel needed to

put on a pot of coffee if they were going to chew that much fat. She had that new gourmet strawberry blend she'd been meaning to try.

Maybe she'd see what Ruth Crisp thought about a little colored child traipsing off to Spain and not returning her mama's phone calls for the past two weeks. And maybe she'd find some way to start bringing up the houseburning, because she was going to have to tell it eventually: Why, it sure seemed a lot of black men were going crazy these days, didn't it, drive-by shooting one another and joining gangs (and burning down each other's $1.1 million houses in the suburbs)?

That bad Freddy Hurd was back, living with his mama and looked like he might be on drugs—they would definitely need to discuss that situation. Mabel hadn't chewed fat like fat was supposed to be chewed in quite some time. She pushed back her chair and stood, and somehow she felt like she was stepping off a shaky platform. She cracked the kitchen window and stood there a moment letting the humidity wash her face. Yes. Let that good smell of rain come on in and make itself at home alongside everyone else.

ABOUT THE AUTHOR

ERIKA ELLIS lives in Santa Monica, California. This is her first novel.

A B O U T   T H E   T Y P E

This book was set in Times Roman, designed by
Stanley Morison specifically for *The Times* of Lon-
don. The typeface was introduced in the newspaper
in 1932. Times Roman had its greatest success in
the United States as a book and commercial typeface, rather than one used in newspapers.